# INTERNATIONAL PRAISE FOR
## *THE ARDENT SWARM*

"Yamen Manai . . . speaks with the accuracy of the scientist and at the same time with the fire of the poet and the imagination of the novelist."
—Jean-Marie Gustave Le Clézio, in interview with Patrick Simonin, TV5 Monde

"[*The Ardent Swarm* explores] the problems of contemporary Tunisia but [they are] approached in a very gentle, very subtle way, with a smile."
—Yvan Le Perec, France Bleu

"What a wonderful little book that is at once an enchantment, a hymn to nature, a warning about intolerance and the fundamentalism that threatens us, and also a great lesson in courage."
—Gérard Collard, La Griffe Noire

# The
# Ardent
# Swarm

# The Ardent Swarm

a novel

# Yamen Manai

Translated from the French
by Lara Vergnaud

AMAZON **CROSSING**

Excerpt from "Anger" in "Selections from the Bestiary of Leonardo Da Vinci," trans. Oliver Evans, Vol. 64, No. 254, of the *Journal of American Folklore*, is used with permission from the American Folklore Society (www.afsnet.org).

Previously published as *L'amas ardent* by Éditions Elyzad in Tunisia in 2017. Translated from French by Lara Vergnaud. First published in English by Amazon Crossing in 2021.

Lara Vergnaud gratefully acknowledges the generous support of a PEN/Heim Translation Fund Grant toward the translation of this book.

Published by Amazon Crossing, Seattle

www.apub.com

Amazon, the Amazon logo, and Amazon Crossing are trademarks of Amazon.com, Inc., or its affiliates.

ISBN-13: 9781542020473 (hardcover)
ISBN-10: 1542020476 (hardcover)

ISBN-13: 9781542020459 (paperback)
ISBN-10: 154202045X (paperback)

Cover design by Adil Dara

Printed in the United States of America

First edition

*And thy Lord taught the Bee*
*to build its cells in hills*
*on trees, and in [men's] habitations;*
*Then to eat of all*
*the produce [of the earth],*
*and find with skill the spacious*
*Paths of its Lord: there issues*
*from within their bodies*
*a drink of varying colours,*
*wherein is healing for men:*
*verily in this is a Sign*
*for those who give thought*

Quran, "The Bee," 16:68–69

# CHAOS

# PROLOGUE

The 320-foot-long yacht left Sardinia early in the morning. Apart from the crew, sober by obligation, everybody on the boat was hungover, and no one spared the hunt for their undergarments upon waking. The prince nudged the naked bodies out of his way, slipping on a silk robe, and navigated between stiletto heels and a sex toy here and there. As he stumbled through the mess, his feet got tangled in a large pair of satin Mickey Mouse briefs, prompting flashbacks to the previous night. He shook the briefs off with a big smile and continued toward the bridge. The sun was strong. As soon as he was spotted, one of his servants rushed to bring him sunglasses, coffee, and a cigar.

The ship sliced through the Mediterranean like a conquistador's galleon. The cliffs of Sidi Bou would be visible by early evening. Despite the idyllic setting, the prince was traveling for work. The only reason they had docked at the quiet port of Santa Teresa di Gallura the night before was that Silvio Cannelloni had been waiting there to talk business.

They certainly didn't lack topics of conversation. Both were influential politicians, presidents of powerful media and telecommunication conglomerates, as well as owners of prestigious European soccer teams. On the agenda for their meeting: Mamar's fate and Thor's transfer. Everything went as planned, followed by Silvio's legendary after-party, the "bonus" that made him so popular. Hell of a guy, the prince thought, texting him on his iPhone: You forgot your boxers again.

The response was immediate: Keep them for Mamar he might need them.

The night before, on the boat, they had discussed Thor's transfer first.

"Let's start with the easy stuff," suggested Silvio.

"Mamar?" replied the prince, feigning ignorance.

"*Cazzo!* Stop fucking around," grumbled Silvio. "No, that's complicated. Let's talk soccer first."

"Whatever you want," laughed the prince. His companion, an aging prime minister, was obsessed with his youth, and the artifices he used to conjure it made for a far-fetched appearance: dyed hair, facelift, Botoxed lips—all wrapped in a suit that was too tight. Silvio was a class act, all right.

"With the salary you promised him, the brute can leave. I can't keep him anymore, but I'm not just going to give him away."

"State your price," said the prince nonchalantly.

Mino Thor was the soccer star of the moment. A behemoth from the North with the looks and manners of a Viking, capable of kicking balls over 125 miles per hour and walking on an opponent on the ground just for the pleasure of humiliating him.

"Sixty million euros, officially, and ten for the pain you're going to cause me. He's an idol in Milan. The *tifosi* are going to rip me apart for months!"

"Deal."

Then they moved on to Mamar's fate.

"I don't agree," Silvio said straightaway.

"We were able to come to an agreement with the tribal chiefs. We'll come to an agreement with you too."

"You're really going to take him out?" asked Silvio.

"It seems inevitable," answered the prince.

"Send him into exile! Look at the Handsome One. He's doing fine in Arabia."

"The Handsome One's washed up. His life isn't worth a thing. Mamar knows too much, and a lot of people have benefited from his money."

"Once he's dead, the Bedouins are going to claim his fortune. His money will be confiscated and his belongings sold for their benefit. That will mean a lot of empty pockets around here!"

"Not all of them," said the prince. "You'll get your part when everything gets seized."

Silvio was in desperate need of money. He had more than a few judges to bribe, plus an election to finance to regain his parliamentary immunity. The deal struck him as fair, and so he reconciled himself. "Poor Mamar. He was nice to me."

"As they say in your country," stressed the prince, "nothing personal. It's strictly business." Silvio nodded in agreement.

The prince continued. "We have to be on the same page, politically and in the international media. We have to drill down the same message, in every opinion column, in the East and the West: the only way to give the Bedouins back their freedom is to topple Mamar, the tyrant persecuting them. Our allies will run the show on the ground."

The Italian let out an impressed whistle. "Our allies will run the show?"

"Absolutely."

The prince didn't say anything else, though the plan had already been hatched. Bounty would charge Mamar's fief from the sea, Nico would parachute weapons over the Bedouins' heads, everyone would get their own Kalashnikov, bullets would fly in every direction, and within this dangerous muddle, Mamar would eventually take a hit. Maybe even a couple. A few in the head . . .

"Perfect," concluded Silvio. He looked at his watch. "I like business that wraps up quickly. Now, let's celebrate!"

The aging politician took out his phone. With one call, the small port was filled with a procession of limousines and models with powdered noses, rivers of brut and rosé champagne, and a spectacular avalanche of multicolored pills. A hell of a guy.

Exhaling the smoke from his Cohiba, the prince stood facing the clear horizon. And even if it hadn't been clear, he would have cleared it. He was the most prominent prince in a crop of royal progeny actively working toward the hegemony and rise of the kingdom of Qafar. That feeling of power sparked a relaxing wave inside him that ran through his body top to bottom, provoking a long, resounding fart along the way.

Even though its size was laughable and its history approximate—the adjectives could easily be switched—Qafar's ambitions had no limit, just like its recently discovered natural gas resources. The deposits were so deep that they would forever change the fate of this small kingdom, once a peaceful village of pearl fishers.

It was no secret that it was gas that gave Qafar its power and its wealth. And when it came to manners in the kingdom, you really didn't have to hold back—the louder and more aromatic the fart, the more applause it garnered from the assembled guests. According to the elders—and in the kingdom of Qafar, the words of the elders were truth itself—the reason this little desert dump had staggering quantities of underground butane was the combination of its people's natural aptitude for farting and the Spartan customs that compelled them to sit ass down on the sand. To the point that, to avoid insulting the conservatives, the first king, Abdul Ban Ania, progressive on certain matters, declared: "There is enough gas underground that we may begin to sit on chairs."

Thus began a modernization effort that left half the planet speechless: a liquefaction industry using cutting-edge technology, skyscrapers planted in the middle of the sea, international news networks of impressive professionalism, and airports for an airline among the best equipped in the world.

Its ambitions spilled over its borders, and in barely ten years, international investments had multiplied, as had the power wielded over the most fragile neighboring countries, which the naysayers called interference. But to hell with the naysayers!

The captain waved at him from the cockpit. The prince pointed to his watch in response.

"We'll be there in four hours," yelled the captain.

"Perfect!"

His appetite was growing.

Soon he'd see the cliffs of Sidi Bou, where other business was waiting for him. Soon this land would fall under the kingdom's control.

The prince wasn't the first to covet this country. Even before its current borders existed, it had been the object of great desire and numerous conquests. Originally a land of Berber tribes, it became, in succession, a shelter for the Phoenicians, a breadbasket for the Romans, spoils for the Vandals, a port for the Byzantines, a paradise for the Arabs, an annex for the Turks, a colony for the Franks . . . Now it was Qafar's turn to take the reins, he thought, rubbing his hands together. Because while the endangered greenery and polluted beaches of this former haven were far from the stuff of dreams, its geostrategic position was still enticing: to both the east and the west were two vast expanses of hydrocarbon that the world's leaders, without exception, had in their sights.

Buying this country square foot by square foot was a whim that his money could allow but that the nation's constitution and international law would not. People have the right to decide their own fate, apparently. Good for them, but was he going to stand idly by? There was no such thing as an impregnable city or an impassable wall. What's more, the circumstances couldn't be more in his favor.

The thing is, after decades of dictatorship, the people here had surprised the Qafaris. They had risen up, waged revolution, and called for self-determination and democracy. About time! What was easier to hijack than democracy? Like most things in the world of men, democracy was principally a question of money, and the prince had plenty.

The first free elections would be held soon, and he had a horse in the race. The Sheik, a local figure, was an eminent member of the religious brotherhood financing the kingdom, whose rigorist doctrine guided his long-underground party—the Party of God. And wouldn't you know it, the revolution had restored the party's image, providing political legitimacy and even bolstering its audience. In the eyes of many, the Party of God had a good chance of winning at the ballot box and seeing its enlightened members make up the first democratically elected government in the country's history.

The prince had anticipated what was needed to bankroll his candidate's march to victory. The yacht's hold was as full as a cargo ship, crammed with boxes of clothes and crates of canned goods. Along with several briefcases of green bills, this was the arsenal of seduction necessary to garner every poor vote, and this country had plenty.

"Here's all you need to fill your booths and go on a nice little tour of the hinterlands. Campaign in the name of God. Distribute the boxes in the name of God and the Party of God," he planned to tell the Sheik during the lovely evening that was approaching.

The models, whom Silvio had left behind, along with his satin briefs, were starting to emerge, one by one, to float in the pool. But they and the prince weren't the only pests. There were even more in the crates stuffed into the yacht's hold.

From time immemorial, the gifts of princes have always been poisoned.

# 1

Everyone knew that Sidi would give his life for his girls, and do so without the slightest hesitation. His love was such that he was capable of anything. Hadn't he devoted his life to them, building them citadel upon citadel? Hadn't he confronted a Numidian bear just to bring them the most beautiful flowers? Hadn't he defied princes and renounced love to dedicate himself entirely to them? And so, when news that many of them had died under troubling circumstances spread from mouth to mouth, a reaction seemed inevitable.

Sidi didn't like to make a show of his problems. He was fairly taciturn by nature, and if the news had circulated through the village of Nawa, it was because, that same morning, little Béchir had been running through the fields as he often did in the early days of spring. When he approached Sidi's colonies, set up on the hill that had the most flowers, he saw the old man on his knees, sobbing before countless mutilated bodies, as the rest of his girls flew around him, as if to console him. Little Béchir was only a child and didn't think to hold his tongue. And so, one hour later, all of Nawa was aware of the tragedy, and all of Nawa was outraged, especially as nobody knew Sidi, much less his girls, to have any enemies. Granted, he was an odd character and could lose his temper at times, but everyone liked him and held him in high esteem. The incident was therefore a complete mystery.

But that didn't stop people from talking about it, which is what they did all day long, recalling seasons past and bemoaning a world going downhill.

"It happened in the middle of the day," maintained Bicha, the hairdresser.

"They were disemboweled, cut in half," lamented Kheira, the village grocer, to Baya, who had come to buy some sugar.

When the village elders were questioned, they went even further. "This is clearly the sign of a curse."

But the collective narrative built around little Béchir's account was merely a stopgap. Everyone was anxious to see Sidi and hear his version of events and his likely conclusions.

As night fell, the fading light outlined Sidi's erect silhouette along the walls of the village. He walked up the narrow alleyways with determination until he reached the terrace of the café where the village men puffed themselves up with hookah smoke and endless conversation. His entrance provoked such silence that nothing could be heard apart from a breeze whistling through the leaves outside and moths repeatedly colliding into the oil lamps. He stopped abruptly and for a moment pondered the compassion-filled faces looking back at him. He continued to his regular table; the voices followed.

"We know what happened. How terrible!"

"All our condolences!"

Sidi nodded soberly in response and pulled out a chair. People had flocked behind him as he walked, and by the time he sat down, he had an entire crowd before him, hanging on his every word.

"How do you all know?"

"Little Béchir."

"Ah, little Béchir, okay. Louz, what are you waiting for? A Turkish coffee, please."

The waiter replied in a lilting voice, "Right away, and with a dash of orange blossom! But don't say anything until I get back."

The gathering held out until the steaming cup was placed before Sidi.

"When did it happen?" asked Louz.

"A little before noon," said Sidi.

"What happened?"

"I don't have the slightest idea. But it wasn't the work of any man or animal from around here," he replied, eliminating any worries in that respect and closing the subject.

The villagers sighed. Some brought up the end of the world while others invoked God's mercy, then, gradually, everyone returned to their seats as games of scopa resumed to the rhythm of hookah pipes and interminable debates. That's how evenings in Nawa went.

# 2

Sidi didn't get any sleep that night. Before camping out beneath his front-door canopy, a vantage point that offered an uninterrupted view of the entire hillside, he had visited his hives, lifting up their lids one by one and observing, by a small sliver of moonlight, their many occupants as they slept. He visited the destroyed hive last, heart sinking as he approached. That very morning, he had discovered the bodies of thirty thousand of his bees at the base of the wooden structure. Most of them ripped to pieces. Thirty thousand bees. Workers. Foragers. Guards. The heart of the hive hadn't been spared. Some unchecked evil had crept all the way to the sacred quarters. The cells were desecrated, the opercula torn, and the larvae ripped from the warmth of their cocoons. And the honey? Not one drop left. It was all gone, like it had been drunk with a straw. And amid the wreckage, the queen. Lethally wounded, feet pointed at the sky in a final prayer. An entire colony destroyed and pillaged in less than two hours' time. A massacre.

Sidi wrapped himself in a blanket and settled into his lounge chair. It was late March, and even though Nawa had landed firmly in spring, the nights were still a little cold. The cicadas hadn't made their appearance yet, and apart from the howls of golden jackals rising in the distance, nothing disturbed the silence. The beekeeper contemplated the fading twilight. The night was melting into a horizon that was disappearing into the sky, and if he happened to lift his eyes, he could see the tips of the pine trees nuzzling the stars. The hives were still visible in the dim light, quiet as dark fortresses, their calm contrasting with that day's feverish state. His colonies had been teeming with bees wilting in the sun. Dawn will come, thought Sidi, but what will it bring? Will the matinal ode to life be the only song, or will it again have a funereal keen? What strange evil had struck the hive, cutting thousands of his girls in two?

His girls. That's how he referred to his bees. All of Nawa knew that and saw the love he felt for them. When it was time for the harvest, the villagers could measure the extent of that passion, savor it even, showing up at Sidi's house at cockcrow to pick up their jars of honey. Conditions were ideal, and the honey produced the just reward for this harmonious relationship between man and nature. The villagers spread nothing but cow dung on their land and pulled up weeds with their own hands. No one dabbled in magic, and they put nothing but sugar in their tea. Far from massive farming operations, from uniform fields and deadly pesticides, the bees around Nawa gathered all kinds of nectars, venturing as far as the woods at the base of the mountain. It was this untamed nature that Sidi, besotted, placed in his jars. And how could he not be besotted with his bees, who had saved him countless times? Their relationship was symbiotic, and he didn't wear protection when visiting his hives. The bees never stung him as they strolled across his hands, even allowing him to caress their plump bellies streaked with honey and rays of gold, their bodies as small and soft as a baby's thumb, delicate legs lightly covered with hair, and wings that gleamed like diamonds whenever the sun flooded the Nawa countryside. Seeing them communicate the best flower patches and thickets was like watching a ballet. They fluttered, grazed, and quivered in a delicate choreography. The dance of life, Sidi had named it, because life advanced thanks to these workers, providing man and animal fruits, nuts, and vegetables, and all the while, offering Sidi divine honey.

And so, for the Nawis, the day when Sidi woke his girls from their winter slumber was a celebration. Once roused, the hives would announce the arrival of spring, bees thronging the surrounding area, though few grumbled upon seeing them. The small blessed creatures flew from flower to flower, pollinating the fields and the forest in a waltz of colors that brightened the eyes and the soul alike. Villagers often found themselves nose to nose with a forager bee that, after writhing haphazardly among the flower pistils, had ended up swathed in various pollens: apricot yellow, apple-tree white, cherry-tree green, and rosemary pink-beige. Sidi always took this as a good omen. And the children of Nawa even said that anyone who saw a bee painted in more than five colors would have their wish granted. When pollination was in full swing, a bee could appear in the most unexpected places.

"I got one of your girls in my teapot today," Borni the mason reported to Sidi one night at the café during a game of scopa. Borni would get bored at his work sites early in the morning and spend the rest of his day in the shade of an olive tree brewing red tea, which he immediately drank, and which in no way prevented him from then taking a nap. "She took a few sips and left. You have to admit that my tea is perfectly sweetened," he bragged.

"Guess who I found in my kitchen, chattering away on the rim of my bottle of almond syrup?" Kheira asked Sidi, when he came to buy matches from her. She was the only grocer in the village, and her grocery store had nothing but the basics. She was also a big talker who expelled words with every breath she took, and she took lots. "Two of your girls. I don't know what they were saying, but I'd have liked to join the conversation!"

And so, when the tragedy struck, everyone felt themselves affected.

# 3

The attack on Sidi's bees wasn't the only odd incident in Nawa's recent history. The previous September, an electoral caravan composed of a dozen cars bearing the national flag made a dramatic entrance to the village. The caravan was just one of many roaming the country's hinterlands, with the goal of adding rural residents to voter lists and setting up voting booths for them. The procession arrived around noon and parked in Nawa's main square with great commotion—grinding motors, beeping horns, singing, ululations. Men and women emerged, most of them young, and visibly enthusiastic. The Nawis forgot their hunger and spontaneously gathered at the small square, which had, without warning, become a site of celebration. The visitors mixed with the natives, as Nawa was still one of those places on earth where you embrace a stranger and ask after their family. After the joy of that first encounter, the time came for explanations. In fact, these men and women had come to explain to the people of Nawa that the world wasn't entirely the same as before and that times had changed. For that matter, one of them thundered into a megaphone, "My dear fellow citizens, times have changed!"

The Nawis looked around but didn't notice anything different. So they asked, "What do you mean, times have changed?"

"From now on, you can choose to be governed by so-and-so or so-and-so."

"Here in Nawa?"

"Here in Nawa, and even at the national level."

The villagers were completely discombobulated. Most of them hadn't even chosen their spouses, and now they were meant to choose who would govern them. Admittedly, some of them had heard, some three months earlier, that something had happened on high, but nobody had understood enough to be able to explain it to the others. Like many modern-day items, newspapers hadn't yet reached Nawa, and even if they had, most of the population was illiterate. The only ones who could read were a few kids who walked for hours across the steppe to go to school. As for television, a likely source of information, there was just the one and it was in the café, and Louz only turned it on for the World Cup, after pestering old man Jbara for months to lend him his cables and the battery from his tractor, the sole motor vehicle in the area. Louz had never bothered to beg old Jbara so he could run the nightly news, since, for a very long time now, the news had been a soap opera with a single episode, during which you saw the Handsome One parade around as journalists tried to come up with new ways to pay him homage.

"So the Handsome One is gone, gone?"

"Absolutely. He's gone and we'll never see him again."

"Like the Old One before him?"

"Not entirely. Remember the Handsome One chased away the Old One and took his place. Now that the people have chased away the Handsome One, it's up to the people to decide who to put in his place."

"And we're the people?"

"Absolutely. Who else would you be?"

The Nawa villagers were delighted to learn that they were the people, though they wondered since when. In their isolation, they had started to believe that they were just the Nawis, and that nobody was interested in their fate, much less their opinions. Nobody had ever asked them anything at all before, and nobody else had been here freezing during harsh winters when they lacked heat, wool, and shoes, and when the sight of little children walking barefoot in the snow broke the hearts of the powerless adults. Nobody came to Nawa. Well, almost nobody.

Admittedly, the day when the Handsome One came to visit them had been a memorable day for all, these Nawis who had been given so little. It was during one of the early years of his reign, shortly after he deposed the Old One. The Handsome One arrived in Nawa like a movie star, in a helicopter, sporting sunglasses. As the improbable machine landed before the dumbstruck villagers, the propellers made such a racket that shepherd Selim's flock fled into the four corners of the valley. The swept-up air hurtled bees into the fields and scattered panicked chickens and straw hats for miles around. The Nawis gathered around the helicopter and watched as cameramen jumped out its doors to immortalize the scene. Once the cameras were rolling, a delegation of black-suited officials emerged from the iron bird and encircled the Handsome One, dripping with class in a gray Hugo Boss suit, shining Hackett shoes, and fashionable Carrera shades covering his eyes. When they saw him, the women spontaneously began to ululate, as if at a wedding. The young people chanted his name, which had just been whispered into their ears, and the most daring adults approached him, offering him the legendary Nawi embrace before the photographers' flashbulbs. The Handsome One was concerned about their destitute condition, and his face had a compassionate air even as his eyes remained completely hidden behind his dark glasses.

"How many families live here?"

"One hundred or so."

"And this village is indeed the village of Nawa?"

"Yes, this is indeed the village of Nawa."

"And why is it called Nawa?"

"This village has been called Nawa for as long as it's existed!"

"Oh really?"

"Since the very first root took hold, this village has been called Nawa."

The Handsome One smiled faintly, then his compassionate expression returned.

"Tell me a little about Nawa."

"This is Nawa, before you, thanks be to God."

"How do you live? Do you have running water? Electricity?"

"No, we don't have any of that. No running water, no electricity. None of that. Thanks be to God."

"And for water, how do you manage?"

"There's a well on the mountain, over there, where we collect water."

The Handsome One looked at the far-off mountain and asked, "How do you get there?"

"With all due respect, on the back of a donkey or a mule."

"Where is the nearest village?"

"The nearest village . . . ," pondered the Nawis. "The nearest village doesn't exist."

"Walou," a member of the delegation whispered to the Handsome One, who continued, "Isn't Walou nearby? How far away is it?"

"It's approximately twelve miles from here."

"Twelve miles. And is there a road?"

"Yes, there's a road," replied the villagers.

The Handsome One looked left and right and saw ramshackle huts, but no road. The only thing connecting Nawa to the neighboring town was the path used by cattle.

"And what's this road like? Not bad . . . ?"

"Yes, not bad." Everyone nodded.

"Or impassable?" continued the Handsome One.

"Impassable! That's it! Impassable! Especially when it rains."

"And did it rain this year? Is the harvest good?"

"The harvest is good, thanks be to God," replied the villagers in chorus.

"And is there an infirmary?"

"No, there's no infirmary."

"And when someone gets sick, what do you do?"

"When it's serious, we take them to Walou."

"And is there a school?"

"Here? No, there's no school."

"And the children, what do they do?"

"Some work alongside us, and some go to the school in Walou."

"All right."

The Handsome One was making a serious face immediately noticed by the journalists, who would mention it in their panegyrics.

"But as long as you are here and you come to see us, everything will be fine, there won't be any problems, thanks be to God," said the villagers.

The Handsome One appeared deeply moved. He left making plenty of promises, and Nawa was the top story on the nightly news. The very next day, a presidential decree mandated the creation of a solidarity fund fed by an obligatory tax. People gave for the Nawis and the like, the forgotten of the earth, but in the end the only ones they were able to save from misery were the Handsome One and his in-laws. For nearly thirty years, nobody talked about the Nawis anymore, and nobody came to visit them again. And so they rode the backs of donkeys in search of water, used oil lamps for light, and made the pilgrimage to Walou—or at least the schoolchildren and the dying did.

But the Handsome One wasn't there anymore. The people had chased him away, and the people had to vote, explained the electoral convoy. They were the people, no rights but plenty of responsibility. A village that still lacked water and electricity, with a handsome premade voting booth set up in the middle of the square.

The caravan left as suddenly as it appeared, leaving behind dust and paper, pounds of leaflets presenting the sixty political parties coveting the comfortable positions created three months prior. And nothing to eat. Nothing to wear.

# 4

It was the last round. Toumi looked at the cards scattered across the table and thought back to the previous hands. Brow furrowed and eyes crinkled in concentration, he silently moved his lips, counting in his head, then yelled out, "Bastard, you have the Seventh Heaven!"

The Seventh Heaven—the seven of diamonds, the most sought-after card in North African scopa. Alone, it's worth one point, and it can gain a player up to two additional points if combined with other cards. For a Nawi, the Seventh Heaven is the best that Heaven can offer.

Douda smiled. Toumi was right. The magical card was indeed in his hand.

"Okay, yes, I'm the bastard with the Seventh Heaven, and you're the bastard with nothing."

But it's not enough to have the Seventh Heaven; you have to make good use of it. Douda looked at the stack, and since there were no favorable combinations, he played another card.

"Stop celebrating over nothing," warned Toumi. "You're going to give the card up eventually. If I was in your position, I'd play it right away. It'll be less painful than losing it in the final hand."

"In my position? Why don't you come take my spot, then?" asked Douda.

Toumi didn't let up. "I don't want to take your spot. I'm just explaining is all. You can't make any more combinations. All that's left is the six of clubs, and there's no more aces. There's no more twos either—they're all gone—so the five in the stack doesn't help you at all."

Douda threw his hand on the table in protest.

"Stop counting cards already! Stop counting cards and let the round play out to the end. Give me some breathing room, damn it!"

Toumi was about to really rub it in by calling Douda a crappy player when he suddenly realized that ruining his friend's pleasure during a game of scopa was what prompted his own, and that when it came to pleasures in life, this was all there was. How depressing, he thought. A naked man undressing a corpse, as the elders would say. He looked down, but the sight of his calloused toes poking out of his old shoes sat him right back up, and he was once again confronted with the appearance of his childhood friend. Disheveled hair, scruffy face, and always the same clothes, ripped in spots and with holes in others. He looked like a disaster survivor. And even though he'd rarely seen himself in the mirror, because in Nawa there was no room for vanity, Toumi knew that Douda was merely the slap-in-the-face reflection of his own hopelessness. He looked away, but his gaze landed on the nearby huts and an arid steppe that stretched in every direction.

What was there to smile about in this godforsaken dump?

He sighed. "In the end, it looks like we're two bastards who've got nothing."

Douda sighed next. "You said it, Toumi, you said it. Two bastards who've got nothing, who're good for nothing."

The sight of the young canvassers from the night before, well dressed, driving cars, able to read, talking about their future, only reminded them of how pitiful they were.

"Come on, let's walk a bit."

They left the café and their feet spontaneously led them to the voting booth. Erect, empty, and closed. A prefabricated unit that the canvassers had put together in barely two hours, and which was by far the most solid construction in the village. It even had a door and windows.

The two men stopped in front of it.

Toumi knocked on the wall, then looked in the windows. "It's more fit to live in than a shack."

Douda still seemed annoyed. The booth didn't appear to be improving his mood. Toumi continued to circle around it.

"They could have set up more of these. We could have lived in them."

"And why exactly would they have done that? Just for your skinny ass?"

"No, it's just that it looks easy enough."

Douda stopped talking. Toumi picked up some pamphlets from the pile set up in front of the door. Neither he nor his friend knew how to read.

"They said that life will be easier if we choose the right people."

"And how do we know who are the right people?"

Toumi looked at the pamphlets in his hands. There were faces, symbols, and writing. These were cards he didn't know how to interpret.

# DISCORD

# 5

The month of October, which would culminate with the nation's first truly democratic elections, didn't merely bring the forager bees' beloved rosemary plants into bloom. The folds of its autumn coat were hiding strange birds that formed a new kind of convoy.

Contrary to the last caravan, primarily composed of young men and women waving the national flag, this one contained bearded men waving a black flag with a white pigeon in the center. Their appearance and way of talking stood out too. The previous canvassers had spoken the local dialect—an imperfect language stigmatized by history—and dressed like city folk, while these new canvassers were decked out in tunics, like the Bedouins of medieval Arabia, though, granted, very few things have evolved in Arabia since the Middle Ages. The nods to that bygone era didn't stop with beards and clothing; these ornaments were enhanced by classical language, full of sacred words, echoing a rigorist rhetoric that the Nawis would soon discover.

These weren't the only differences. Whereas the first convoy's speaker system had broadcast bland, unconvincing patriotic chants, and their car trunks had been packed with pamphlets promising the moon, the loudspeakers of the second caravan emitted decibels of religious chants for the glory of God and the Last Prophet, and the beds of their pickup trucks were filled with crates of food, blankets, and clothes.

The bearded men parked next to the voting booth. Some began to unload the goods while others bellowed into megaphones, reminding their audience of God's greatness, scattering Selim the shepherd's sheep to the four corners of the valley, and attracting another flock composed of Nawis.

"God is great! God is great!"

The Nawis repeated after them, for how could they do otherwise. "God is great! God is great!"

"Come closer, my sisters, come closer, my brothers! Help yourselves! This is for you."

"For us?"

"Yes! Help yourselves."

Blankets, shoes, bags of clothes, bags of rice, boxes of canned food, cartons of soap, crates of meat, crates of vegetables, packets of cookies, and more. Never in their lives had the Nawis been the object of such solicitude; it was as if for one moment Heaven had opened its gates to them. The rush lasted at most half an hour, and then there was nothing left. By the end, on average, each Nawi had made three round trips between the distribution site and their shack, and had collected forty or so pounds of various foodstuffs.

When the villagers returned to the square to thank their bearded benefactors, the latter denied being the source of any charity whatsoever. "My brothers, we are servants of God. We are only doing our duty. It is our duty to come to your aid."

The Nawis were confused. True, the country as a whole called itself a land of believers, some even going as far as to call it a land of saints, but nobody before these visitors had used that as a reason to save his fellow man.

The most heavily bearded member of the assembly, who appeared to be the leader, continued the speech. His head of hair and belly were equally impressive. What's more, the green mark above his eyes left little doubt about the incalculable number of hours he spent in prayer, forehead against the ground. His walleyed gaze, one motionless orb fixed on the horizon, lent him a mystical air, and his melodious voice resonated with emotions, from shrillest to deepest. After having exalted the All-Powerful countless times, and praising His Prophet, the Last Prophet, he said:

"My brothers and sisters, it is I who must thank you from the bottom of my heart. Because of you, today, my day is beautiful, and I have gained a plot in Heaven. What better could befall a man than to prepare his eternal home by following the path of the Eternal in his earthly life? That is the reason I am here among you, with my hand stretched out. God is my choice. His word, my law. So, when the time comes, do as I did, choose God! When the time comes to vote, vote for the Party of God!"

Then the tone of his voice became more instructive and authoritative as he unfolded a paper ballot with multiple boxes next to multiple emblems.

"Once you're in the voting booth, you check here, check the pigeon," he explained.

The pigeon was the emblem of the Party of God.


The week between this visit and the elections was pleasant in the village. At night, the Nawis slept with their bellies full, beneath warm blankets, and when they woke, they dressed in their new tunics. The day of, those who were old enough to vote showed up early and checked the pigeon. All the Nawis. Well, with one exception.

# 6

The reason Sidi had missed this memorable display of civic engagement was that he was far from humankind, exploring, in pine treetops and mountainside burrows, the territory of those bees labeled wild and whom he called free.

These secret spots harbored precious swarms that he would gather to breed new queens, which he then introduced into his colonies. Wild queens are more resistant and more vivacious than their domesticated cousins, and the generations they beget strengthen hives against scourge and disease.

On several occasions, he had used this method to fight parasites, notably the *Varroa destructor*. Their fierce battle had been going on for decades.

A formidable menace, this nonnative acarid, which resembled a crab but was as small as the head of a pin, had overrun hives at the end of the Old One's reign. Like many other scourges that flourished hand in hand with lucrative trades, the *Varroa* took advantage of the commerce in bees, now just another commodity, to legally cross borders. This leech passed through customs astride domesticated European bees, the *Apis mellifera*, which were imported into the country en masse because they were more docile and better producers than the North

African *intermissa*, their bad-tempered local cousins, who had never encountered the parasite.

The newly introduced acarids found themselves ferried to wherever flowers bloomed, easily jumping from one forager bee to another, contaminating the *intermissa*; it only took two decades for the *Varroa* to strike every hive in the country. As with every curse, the victim was also the vehicle for conquest and expansion.

Though it had arrived in the time of the Old One, the *Varroa* prospered in the era of the Handsome One, like many of its kin. There wasn't one worker bee in a field without this parasite on its back, hooks planted in its flesh. Not only did the leech suck the bee dry, it also infected its host with contagious and deadly diseases, which would eventually destroy the entire hive.

In their fight against the *Varroa*, many beekeepers converted to pesticides to save their colonies, preserving life with the right dose of poison. Except that with poison, there is no right dose.

Sidi's hives, which had also been infected, survived on their own. Bolstered by the introduction of wild queens, they hadn't succumbed. His bees knew how to defend themselves against the *Varroa* at every stage of their development, and, to do so, showed their savage side. They had inherited a sense of smell once lost through servile domestication and could recognize the odor of parasitic nymphs, which they would then tear apart before expelling the contaminated alveoli. And if they detected an enemy astride an adult bee, they immediately set to get rid of it. Joining forces, the bees would rip the intruder off like plucking a flea off a head, then expel it quick as can be.

But when Sidi set out on that much-vaunted election day to explore pine treetops and mountainside burrows, it wasn't to refortify his hives against parasites. This time, the signs of weakness shown by his bees were entirely endogenous. For a while now, when the sun was at its peak and its light at full strength, his girls had been in distress. Disoriented, they would hesitate on the landing pad, launch into unusual dances, and on multiple occasions, a handful would enter a hive other than their own. As soon as the sun went down, the light faded in intensity, and some shade returned, the flock returned to normal.

It was the first time in his life as a beekeeper that he had seen such a phenomenon.

Seeking the answer in nature, he noticed on his walks that wild bees didn't fear direct sunlight. On the contrary, it was at noon that their dances were the most beautiful and the most perfect.

Had the shade of their artificial hives affected his girls' vision, gradually rendering them photosensitive? This was the only explanation he could find. If he introduced wild queens into the brood, his bees should regain their full capacity to situate themselves in space and time.

Whenever he set out to find wild queens, or simply to get water from the spring, Staka was Sidi's preferred companion. He had purchased the gray donkey several winters ago, at the livestock market in Walou. Sidi had noticed him among the others of his species because his eyes contained a gentleness absent in the gazes of many men, starting with the one who sold him the donkey. Staka never balked at his tasks, though he went at his own rhythm, which worked out well, since Sidi was never in a hurry. And when, after a hard day of service, Sidi placed a sugar cube in the palm of his hand to reward him, Staka would inhale it instantly. His nostrils would quiver, and his thick lips would shake as if he were laughing.


In the quiet of the breaking dawn, Sidi stretched his stiff legs and took a deep breath. Dew was dripping down the leaves, and in the distance, the mountain was starting to take on muted colors as its slopes and scarps slowly emerged from shadow. This was where the most beautiful forager bees in the region could be found. The ones that didn't shy from the light and on which the *Varroa* had no hold.

It would take Sidi half a day to reach his destination, and if he was able to find a large swarm quickly, he could get back before nightfall.

He filled his water gourd, wrapped some bread and olives in a cloth, attached the cart to Staka's back, tightened the buckles around his flanks, and loaded him with a double ladder, his toolbox, and an empty hive. They took the road heading west, where the towering mountain reached its peak.


After an hour, as the end of the steppe came into view, he heard the sound of tires and engines coming up the road. It's not time for the patrol, he rightly noted. Usually, the guards made their rounds at nightfall: that was the moment awaited by wolves and vampires, primed on both sides of the border, to jump out of the darkness. Sidi didn't know that now the guards also patrolled in the morning since, as of late, wolves had begun to circulate in broad daylight, and vampires could tolerate sun and light.

The sound came closer and three jeeps of border guards approached. The convoy slowed down. The first jeep matched its speed to the donkey's. A guard called to him through an open window, *"Salam, Haj!"*

Sidi tipped up his straw hat and looked at the guard out of the corner of his eye. He could make out four young men, boys really, in the vehicle wearing military fatigues. He had a bad feeling. These uniforms made him think of war, death, and blood. He responded, "You call me *haj* even though I've never seen the Kaaba?"

The young soldier was surprised. Ordinarily, old men were flattered by the distinction, claimed if the pilgrimage had been made, or considered a good omen if not. He responded, embarrassed, "One day, *inshallah!*" God willing.

Sidi lowered his hat and said in a tone that left no room for discussion, "When hens have teeth."

The soldier looked even more surprised. He glanced at his comrades, as if seeking backup, and they all burst into laughter.

"You hear that? When hens have teeth! Is that what he just said?"

He turned back to Sidi and tossed out, "Have a nice day all the same!"

The beekeeper waved. The convoy picked up speed and passed him, voices echoing behind. "Crazy old man!"

Staka brayed but Sidi reassured him. "Don't get upset, Staka. They might be right."

They began to climb the first slope. There was brush everywhere. For an interloper, it was a trap of climbing plants and thorns, but Staka and Sidi knew every recess. Budding rosemary carpeted the ground, and the entire mountain exhaled its invigorating scent into the air. Birdsong mixed with the cracking of trees and a chorus of insects that included Sidi's girls, who were playing their notes to perfection. They were capable of venturing far in their sacred quest, and he often encountered them a two-hour walk away.

Staka tugged, making Sidi sway in his cart, more satisfied than a maharajah on his elephant. Although there had been several dry seasons in a row, the scrubland hadn't lost its coat, and its undemanding vegetation offered a sumptuous landscape painted in the colors of autumn.

The expedition advanced over a bed of clover in the shade of oak and pine trees.

Sidi couldn't see his girls anymore. They were now out of their pollen-gathering range. This was their wild sisters' territory.

"If we don't find them in a tree trunk, we'll have to go looking in the caves."

Staka nodded his head as if to indicate that he knew what to expect. The man and his animal were no longer in the prime of youth, and finding a swarm among the rocks was not a risk-free undertaking.

The morning passed in this way, a peaceful hike, senses on alert, alternating between expert scrutiny and enthralled contemplation.

After a quick lunch and a fifteen-minute nap, Sidi resumed his quest.

"Veer left, friend," he said. "Let's head toward the rocks."

On the path, Sidi sat up straight and Staka stopped abruptly.

"You hear that, Staka? Do you hear that buzzing?"

Staka pricked up his long ears and wriggled his thick lips. Sidi got off the cart and advanced on foot, inspecting the flora as his servitor followed.

"Glorious buzzing"—he lifted his head and looked around—"that's what I hear. Glorious buzzing!"

As he advanced, his gaze flickered in multiple directions, following golden dots in the sky.

"Do you see them, flying everywhere?"

Staka confirmed by flicking his ears.

"Old friend, I think what we have here are bees looking for a home!"

That's what happens when a bee kingdom is overpopulated. Some of the inhabitants leave to establish a new one. This small swarm temporarily settles in a high branch while scouts are sent to nearby areas to find a new home. When one finds an ideal spot, it returns and performs a vibrating dance. Beating its wings and wiggling its stomach, the scout communicates the location and its characteristics to the entire swarm. The bees then migrate in a cloud to their new dwelling—generally a narrow cavity or the inaccessible interior of a tree trunk.

At the base of an Aleppo pine, Sidi delighted at what he saw. "There you are, my darlings!"

The bees were massed together on a single branch, one atop the other, quivering in unison. They were indeed in transit, searching for a home, and the vibrating swarm they formed, naked and exposed, gave the impression of a heart beating in nature's open chest.

Without bothering with tools or a suit, Sidi took the ladder from the cart, opened it, and set it against the tree. This swarm was a gift from nature. No need to clear a way through the woods or navigate the rocks. He wasn't going to drive out the bees, but he would offer them a habitat. And so they would be less aggressive with him.

"Stay there, Staka."

He climbed up, the hollow hive hanging around his neck like a vendor's tray. For a long time he had been capable of carrying out the work of three men alone. Today, he remained convinced that was true and conceded nothing to time, even if he surprised himself by taking more precautions than before.

"What you lose in strength, you gain in clear-sightedness. The trick is to reach the age of wisdom while you're still strong enough to do things."

Once level with the swarm, he took the time to admire it.

"Hello, my beauties. Looking for a new house, huh? That works out nicely—I have one all ready for you."

Facing the bees, hive extended below them, Sidi yanked on the branch. The swarm fell, landing with a thud in the gaping hive. The cluster disintegrated into little bees weaving in and out of the honeycomb frames. A few minutes later, they had taken possession of their new quarters.

Meanwhile, Sidi, perched on his ladder, was performing a balancing act. The weight of the hive had now doubled, but his deep breathing was helping him keep it upright. Under Staka's attentive gaze, he carefully descended. Once on the ground, he set down his load and began stretching to revive his stiff joints. Then he settled on the grass, drank a few sips of water, and took out the bread and olives.

# 7

The art of breeding queens lies in making the worker bees think that their empress has disappeared. Panic-stricken upon sensing her absence from the hive, they rapidly breed new queens. They feed a dozen larvae royal jelly, the ultimate honey, a rare substance created solely for this grand occasion. Though a worker bee will make an entire spoonful of honey in her lifetime, she will produce no more than a bead of royal jelly, and that only when necessary.

Any larva fed on royal jelly becomes a queen. When several contenders emerge from their opercula, they fight for supremacy of the colony until one remains. As soon as the new monarch is crowned, she roams the frames, making her way among her subjects and releasing calming scents to restore harmony in the hive. Later, she'll unfurl her wings for the nuptial flight. She will be followed by a cloud of drones, the hive's only males, wanting to fertilize her. The winners of this contest are few and pay for their glory with their lives. Once the queen returns to the colony, she will lay as many as two thousand eggs a day, thereby ensuring her legacy.

Standing before the hive of wild bees that he recovered two weeks earlier, the artist began.

Sidi filled his smoker with wet leaves and added some embers. He attached the nozzle and then pumped the bellows several times. Blast after blast, the smoke came out dense, cold, and odorless.

The beekeeper announced himself by lightly knocking on the hive wall. The guard bees flew out to meet him.

"Hello, my beauties, apologies for the intrusion."

They flitted around him, consenting.

"So, happy with your new home?" he asked, lifting the roof. "Perfect. You all look nicely settled in to me."

To limit their flight, he spread the smoke from the bellows above the honeycomb frames. The worker bees remained frozen in place, thinking there was a fire. The most curious among them took a step back.

"I'm sorry, my beauties. Personally, if I was a little bee, I'd hardly appreciate some man coming to smoke me out. But believe me, it's for a good cause, and deep down, I feel more like a bee than a man."

One by one, he removed the frames from the brood chamber and inspected the small world swarming before him, so dense that it was difficult to distinguish individuals. The bees were circulating in every direction, driven by an exuberance of energy. No time for false niceties or petty squabbles. Each bee knew that they were fellow creatures working for the good of all, and none got upset if jostled or pushed. Not even the queen. They formed a single body.

"There's her majesty."

He had the expert eye and had identified her easily. Larger than the others, her abdomen entirely golden, the queen gave off a benevolent aura as she weaved among her subjects. Sidi picked her up delicately.

"Hello, my queen."

He looked at her with admiration. Out in the sunlight, she shone like a jewel. Her thin legs were shaking, and her stinger was extended, the ultimate sign of protest.

"I know," he consoled her. "I took you from your hive, but there's another one impatiently awaiting you, one that's eager for you to help it see clearly again."

He placed her in a jar and put back the frame and the roof. The bees began to sense her cruel absence, and their buzzing grew louder.

"Yes, my little orphans," sympathized Sidi. "Don't worry. You'll get through this, and you'll raise new monarchs."

He then headed toward his old hives. Standing in front of the colony that displayed the greatest weakness when exposed to direct sunlight, the alchemist continued his ritual.

Once again, he found and deposed the colony's queen, isolating her in a second jar. As the hive buzzed its displeasure, he took out the wild queen and enthroned her. After a few hesitant steps, during which she was surrounded and jostled by a curious, swelling crowd, the new queen successfully established herself through her dance and her scent. She was unanimously accepted by her new subjects, and the buzzing of protest turned to purring. Harmony returned to the citadel. The worker bees resumed flight. Soon the queen would lay her eggs in this brood, teasing out its memories and awakening a legacy buried in their genes, hidden over time by domestic life in the shadow of cities.

This legacy would be reintroduced into all of Sidi's colonies. For two weeks, his orphaned bees would dedicate themselves to transforming a dozen larvae into royal nymphs. The beekeeper would supervise their development in the cells the whole time. When they hatched, he would keep one as queen and remove the others before, out of instinct, they tore each other apart. One by one, he would enthrone them in the different broods of his apiary, at the expense of the old monarchs. His art and his expertise would bring to life generations capable of braving the test of the midday sun.

# 8

One week in, Sidi found himself out of matches. He untied Staka and headed to Nawa. Matches were one of the rare supplies abundantly available in Kheira's little store.

The village was located at the base of his hill, which, at most, took him half an hour to reach. A quick trip, he thought as he tightened his burnoose, even though he knew that Kheira was a hell of a talker and you had to be clever to get out of her unending conversations. He never could have imagined that he would end up encouraging her to talk, granting her his full attention in exchange.

When he reached the village, he tied up his donkey and went to the grocery shop on foot. When he saw the Nawis, he rubbed his eyes, incredulous.

Where on earth am I? he wondered.

The women were dressed in black from head to toe, and the men, who had given free rein to their beards, were outfitted with long tunics and tight skullcaps. Everyone who greeted him did so by reciting prayer upon prayer about prophets he knew and others he didn't. Nothing was familiar anymore. Sidi felt an instant surge of worry.

He ran to the shop in search of refuge.

But the shopkeeper's appearance did little to reassure him.

Trusty Kheira had traded her legendary red scarf with Berber designs for a satiny black veil that made her look like a widow.

"Oh, how nice to see you! Where have you been holed up? We haven't seen you in weeks!"

"That you, Kheira?" he asked skeptically.

"Who else would it be?! Don't you recognize me?" she responded indignantly.

"Of course I do. Grab me a carton of matches."

Kheira got on her stepladder, grumbling. "Of course I do! Yeah right, of course you don't! You should come down more. You'll end up not recognizing anybody anymore. If we were bees, you'd visit us more often!"

"You're right on two counts. You're not bees, and I won't be able to recognize anyone anymore. But come on, where'd this"—he pointed to her ensemble—"come from?"

"What? My new clothes? Oh, that's right! You missed the big handout."

"The big handout?"

That's all Kheira needed to happily launch into a recap worthy of a big-time reporter. She didn't omit a single detail, moving her account along with a few "you knows?" and a couple "if only you knews!" She told him about the arrival of the first caravan of canvassers who had told them about the fall of the Handsome One before setting up a premade voting booth and handing out truckloads of pamphlets. Then she described the visit by the bearded benefactors who spoke of God in highly polished terms while filling the villagers' huts with food, clothes, and blankets.

"They handed out stuff in the name of God?" he asked, confused.

"And we accepted everything in the name of God!" she answered, kissing the two sides of her hand.

The matter struck him as shifty.

"Without asking for anything in exchange?" asked Sidi.

Kheira thought for a bit.

"No, they did!" she said, pulling out a folded piece of paper that she laid on the counter. It was a sample ballot, already filled out.

"On election day," she continued, "the holy man said to check here. Check the pigeon!"

Sidi bent over the paper, and instead of a pigeon printed in ink he saw a crow of ill omen.

"Oh really? That's all the holy man said?" he repeated, looking more closely. Then he stood up. "And when are these elections exactly?"

"In a few days. We're all going. Will you come?"

"I'm a man with no debts," he answered, paying for the carton. "I'm off. I have things to do."

"Let's get out of here," he said as he untied Staka from the tree.

The donkey sensed his master's distress and set off.

What were these beards and tunics, this bizarre vocabulary, these new attitudes doing here? He had lived in this kind of world once before, and he had returned forever changed.

# 9

Douda, riding a mule, stopped in front of Toumi's hut.

"Toumi, come out of your shithole!"

Toumi didn't take long to emerge, preceded by his two goats and the pack of hens and chicks that shared his roof day and night.

"I'm going to Walou to buy some fish. Want to come?"

Hand shading his eyes, Toumi looked at his friend framed in the light.

"You got what you need to buy fish?"

Douda indicated two burlap bags overflowing with prickly pears, attached to the sides of his steed.

"If I can sell these, I'm going to buy one beautiful fish."

Looking at the bags filled to the brim, Toumi wondered by what miracle they could sell everything in one day. Prickly pear cactuses grew all over the region and, consequently, their fruits, nicknamed "sultans," were worth nothing on the scale. There had to be some thirty kilos of them. As he made the mental calculation, Toumi imagined the trouble his friend had gone to finding the sultans one by one amid the thorns. Thirty kilos at half a dinar per kilo would make a fifteen-dinar profit, which, as he recalled, was the price per kilo for fish. Good old Douda, he thought, working hard, despite the December cold, to pick the last fruits left behind by men and late fall, and hoping for nothing but *baraka*, a divine blessing.

"Let's go!"

Toumi untied his mule, climbed on, and the two friends took the road to town, a good two hours away.

Douda looked tired, and his hands, riddled with spines, were just barely holding onto the reins. His gaze was pensive.

"The fish is for Hadda," he said.

"Good move."

"She's pregnant."

Toumi started astride his mule. "That's great news! Congratulations, Douda!"

Douda stared resignedly at his delighted friend.

"She's four months pregnant. You know her, she's not difficult. But lately all she dreams about is fish. And you know what they say—a pregnant woman who doesn't satisfy her food cravings will bring an unlucky child into the world."

Toumi tried to cheer up his friend. "Enjoy it and stop worrying. We'll get her that fish!"

Douda didn't appear to have heard him.

"She dreams of eating sea bream braised on the *kanoun*. How does she even know that there's a fish called the sea bream? Sometimes she really surprises me."

Toumi furrowed his brow. He didn't know any fish other than canned tuna and canned sardines.

"And it's not the cheapest one," sighed Douda. "We're going to have to sell every last one of these sad sultans."

They reached Walou midmorning.

The town was teeming with locals and visitors alike, cars and carts battling for road space with pedestrians and animals. The Nawi duo tied up their mules and set up at the market entrance. As Douda slumped in exhaustion, Toumi took charge. He unloaded the merchandise, presented it as best he could, and began to shout, "Eight sultans for one dinar! Eight sultans for one dinar!"

When the muezzin announced the midday prayer, they had only made three dinars.

They left to pray. When in Walou, they never skipped a prayer because it was their only opportunity to wash up, thanks to the faucets available in the mosque restroom. Douda prayed with all his heart to the Most Generous for a small sea bream so that Hadda wouldn't bring an unlucky child into the world.

But the afternoon didn't go much better than the morning, so much so that Douda lowered his aims accordingly. "Twelve sultans for one dinar! Twelve sultans for one dinar!"

The new price brought in a few more clients but not enough. At the end of the day, they were left with seven dinars and half a bag of sultans on their hands. Little by little, the market closed down. The merchants began to pack up their stalls.

"But we have a Seventh Heaven!" said Toumi. "It must be worth something. Hurry up, before the fish merchants clear out."

Douda followed him, clutching the dinars like a talisman in his scarred hand. On the way, they passed the produce section, where fruits considered nobler than the sultan reached exorbitant prices per kilo. The vegetables weren't spared either. Everything had shot up in price. For many, any plans of cooking a piece of meat came to an end in the butchers' aisle. Douda advanced reluctantly. He was scared to continue, and his steps grew heavy. He told himself that a man who can barely afford two kilos of bananas couldn't hope to buy sea bream. But Toumi didn't seem to realize any of this and marched straight ahead. As they got closer, they picked up the smell of the sea, and the cats began to outnumber the people. Meowing with frustration at the entrance to the fish merchants' territory, the most adventurous felines earned nothing but a stern kick.

The fish were displayed at angles in piles of ice, smooth and glistening, in different sizes, shapes, and colors. But they were all goggle-eyed with mouths wide open, as if stunned to see the two Nawis appear before their majestic stand.

Behind their wares, the fish merchants stood on large platforms, which made them look considerably taller. Sporting nitrile aprons, rubber gloves, and plastic boots up to their knees, the overall impression was of torturers. Douda felt so small and pathetic that he could no longer speak.

"Which ones are the sea bream?" asked Toumi.

With a trembling finger, Douda pointed at a silvery pile. A sign indicated a price of thirty dinars per kilo. Toumi had trouble believing it.

"That's impossible. There must be a mistake."

He asked the vendor, "Hey, pal, how much per kilo?"

The fish seller bent over and identified the object he was eyeing.

"The sea bream? Thirty dinars!"

"Thirty dinars per kilo?!" Toumi whistled.

"It's sea bream, not pool bream," explained the fish seller. "Farmed bream is half price, but I don't have any left."

Toumi had never been in the sea or a pool, so the man's explanations did little to satisfy him. The Nawi bristled. "So? What a scam!"

Visibly outraged, the seller descended from his stand. It turned out there was nothing gigantic about him. He was an old fisherman with skin tanned by sun and salt.

"Do you think that I'm eating any of the fish that I catch? You know how much it costs me to go out to sea and bring back fish on ice all the way to Walou? I have no doubt there's still people running scams in this country, but they're not here!"

As Toumi, confused, mumbled an apology, Douda broke his silence. "Look, what can I have for seven dinars?"

"A couple red mullets."

He resigned himself. "Weigh out that amount."

"I'll tell her it's sea bream," he whispered to Toumi.

As they were preparing to leave, the muezzin announced the sunset prayer. The two friends looked at one another, then headed back to the mosque. A crowd of young men was restlessly queuing at the door, like the first day back to school. Like the Nawi duo, they had grown out their beards and were wearing tunics and skullcaps, undoubtedly obtained during another big handout.

"What's going on? Why are there so many people?" Douda asked a man organizing entry to the prayer room.

Though overwhelmed, the man responded in a fraternal tone. "It's the sunset prayer, my brothers, like every night! Come, find a spot."

"The sunset prayer?" puzzled Toumi.

"Like every night?" puzzled Douda.

They knew about the Friday prayer. However, neither of them knew that there were now prayers at sunset, and at nearly every hour of the day.

Douda pulled Toumi's hand. "We don't have time. It'll be night soon, and there's not even a crescent of a moon to light our way back."

But the man they had questioned held them forcefully by the shoulders and urged them. "Stay, my brothers! Stay and listen. A holy man will be speaking."

And he pushed them inside.

# CONFUSION

# 10

Douda and Toumi took their places in the ranks. They learned from their neighbors that the holy man was the new imam of Walou, tasked with preaching by the Ministry of Religious Affairs, itself restructured from top to bottom since the Party of God had won the national elections.

Seated in the *mihrab*, the man was facing the crowd, which was kneeling with ears wide open. He coughed lightly, chased the frogs and devils from his throat, lifted his hands to the sky, and thundered: "Glory be to God the All-Powerful, and may praises blanket His Prophet, the Last in Name!"

"Glory be to God the All-Powerful, and may praises blanket His Prophet, the Last in Name!"

"My brothers, settle in and listen to my words. They are important words, so listen closely and listen to the end, for he who listens, whatever he did before, will see the list of his sins purged soon enough. My brothers, come closer to me, and God will bring you closer to Him in the afterlife. Repeat after me: Glory be to God the All-Powerful, and may praises blanket His Prophet, the Last in Name!"

The crowd repeated the holy man's words several more times until he was satisfied. He raised his hands and silence reigned.

"I've seen people turn toward he who has gold.

"And turn away from he who does not!

"I've seen people take interest in he who has money.

"And lose interest in he who does not!

"I've seen people go wild for he who has diamonds.

"And go cold for he who does not!

"My brothers, I'm going to tell you a story. A story that took place in our country—and recently, I should add. A story of two brothers, one rich and one poor. The rich brother was a sheep farmer and had an enormous flock. He shared nothing, not even with his own brother. Worse! He let him rot in misery. One day, the poor brother was sitting outside, leaning against a wall with his son. No one came to see them or ask about their circumstances. They were avoided, in fact, like lepers, while across the street, the wealthy brother was holding a massive feast packed with people. Between two mouthfuls, the rich farmer sneezed, and without even giving thanks to God, he continued eating. Nonetheless, men came running from the end of the street to bless him.

"'May God bless you! May God bless you!' they told him, kissing his hand and begging for a spot at the feast.

"God made it so that at the same time the rich brother sneezed, the poor brother sneezed, and when he did, he gave Him thanks. And yet, nobody came to bless him.

"His son pointed this out. 'Father, nobody came to bless you even though men from all over came to bless my uncle.'

"'Son,' answered the poor man, 'God blesses the man of good deeds, and men bless the man of many sheep!'

"My brothers, that's what matters in people's eyes today—money! But tell me, was the Chosen One rich? Answer me! Was the Last in Name wealthy?"

Heads moved like a pendulum.

"No. The Chosen One was not rich!"

"The Chosen One only had two changes of clothing," he thundered, "and he slept on the ground itself! May the prayers of God be upon him. Repeat after me, my brothers: May the prayers of God be upon him."

"May the prayers of God be upon him!" repeated the crowd, in chorus.

"When he died, my brothers, the Last Prophet had seven bronze coins and one mule. How many bronze coins did he have? How many?"

"Seven!"

The imam nodded his head.

"Seven bronze coins, my brothers, and one mule. My brothers, praise the Lord!"

"Glory to God the All-Powerful!"

"Seven bronze coins! The Last Prophet didn't live in a palace. He didn't have a house on the coast. He didn't have luxury cars, and he didn't wear gold or diamond jewelry. And in his lifetime, he did not eat lavish meals. And my brothers, who is the example for us to follow? Those greedy men who amass things and riches, building castles and houses, who care little about their home in the eyes of the Eternal? Are these the examples to follow?"

Heads moved like a pendulum. "No, these are not the examples to follow!"

"Of course not! The only example to follow in this world is the Last Prophet, may God's praises be upon him!"

"May God's praises be upon him!"

"Good, my brothers, but do you know why the Chosen One accorded so little importance to appearances and material things? God said it. The Chosen One said it! Do you know what he said?"

Heads moved like a pendulum. "No, we don't know what he said!"

The imam nodded. "The Chosen One said, 'God does not see in you your image or your fortune, but your hearts and your deeds.' Your hearts and your deeds! What does God see in us? Repeat after me: Our hearts and our deeds!"

"Our hearts and our deeds!"

"For that, my brothers, let's take inspiration from the first companions. These were men of pure hearts and guided actions, so much so that the Prophet told them in their lifetimes of their accession to Paradise. But do you know where the Chosen One's companions died? Go on, tell me where they died! Tell me where they were buried!"

"We don't know where they died!"

"After the Chosen One's death, the companions left to spread the faith to the four corners of the world. The most illustrious of them died in Anatolia, another, equally illustrious, died in Central Asia, and another in North Africa. None of the Chosen One's companions died at home or were buried in their gardens. Do you know why? Do you?"

The crowd shook their heads. "No, we don't know why."

"My brothers, none of the companions died at home because they all took the path of God to spread His message, inform those who did not yet know, convince those who were not yet convinced, and fight those who did not want to listen. The oldest of the companions, Abu Kalta, was a holy man. What was his name? What was it?"

"Abu Kalta!" echoed the room.

"Abu Kalta was a holy man. He died almost twenty-five hundred miles away from home, on the route to India. Despite his advanced age, he attended every battle and was the first to brandish the holy banner. During his final missions, he had difficulty getting on a horse, and he asked his companions to strap him to his steed because he lacked the strength to squeeze its flanks. And when his hour came, as he was on his deathbed, he uttered his last wishes. Do you know what his last wishes were? Do you know?"

"No, we don't know."

The preacher had tears in his eyes, and his voice fluttered.

"The old companion asked for the banner to be attached to his body, and for his body to be attached to a powerful horse that would be allowed to run through the Indian jungle, so that he could expand the kingdom of God even after his death. Praise God, my brothers!"

"God is great!"

"My brothers, do you know what reward awaits he who takes the road of God to expand His kingdom? His nightly prayer counts as seven hundred thousand ordinary prayers, though this same prayer made in a holy place is worth only one hundred thousand ordinary prayers. Can you imagine, my brothers, the reward that God holds in store for he who takes His path? Men of science say that the Almighty doubles the reward for good deeds on the day of the Last Judgment. Do you know how much that makes in total? Tell me how much that makes. Tell me!"

The preacher caught his audience unprepared, for nobody was good enough at math to simultaneously imagine so many zeros and multiply them by two. But since he had already made the calculation, he was swift to impress them.

"That makes one million four hundred thousand ordinary prayers for just one nightly prayer made on the path of God! One million four hundred thousand prayers! That is true wealth, my brothers! Glory be to God Almighty! Repeat after me: Glory be to God Almighty!"

"Glory be to God Almighty!" repeated the crowd in chorus.

The imam nodded.

"My brothers, I'm going to tell you a good one, about the Chosen One's companion who conquered the northern tip of Africa, may he be praised. At the time, this place was a jungle. The barbarians were living here, as well as all manner of wild beasts. Lions, elephants, and panthers, like there are now in the land of the Blacks. There were even snakes of considerable size, capable of swallowing a man in a few minutes. Six missions and six failures, and the word of God had yet to spread through the region. The barbarians were ferocious and nature untamed. Then the conquest was entrusted to a seventh man, Abu Tassa. What is his name? What is it?"

"Abu Tassa!"

"Abu Tassa, my brothers, may he be praised. He was one of the last companions, a man of unshakable faith, and it was with his faith that he braved the jungle. For three days and three nights, accompanied by men with strong voices, he shouted as loud as he could: 'Oh animals of the jungle! We have come to deliver the Word of God. Do not stand in our way!' Believe it or not, my brothers, at the end of the third day, they saw the animals leave the jungle and head south, to take refuge in the land of the Blacks! Gorillas jumping from tree to tree, lionesses with their cubs in their mouths, giant snakes weaving every which way! Do you believe it or not? Say that you believe it! Say it!"

"Yes, we believe it!" answered the crowd in chorus.

"Glory be to God, my brothers! According to Abu Tangara, who recounted that Abu Chankara heard Abu Fantacha say, 'I heard Abu Machmacha say that he heard the Chosen One say: If you take the path of God, God will put fear *in* all that see you. But if you don't take the path of God, He will put the fear *of* all within you.' What do you prefer, my brothers, being feared by all or being frightened of all? Man, animals, and even demons cannot touch a man who has taken the path of God! Glory be to God, my friends! Repeat it!"

"Glory be to God," repeated the crowd in chorus.

"But if you take the path of God, you no longer belong to yourself. You belong to Him! You belong to Him and you already have one foot in Paradise. You are no longer of this world but of a world between the Two Worlds! You no longer belong to your house, you no longer belong to your wife, you no longer belong to your children, you no longer belong to your country . . . God calls you, and you took His path, you stand beside His angels, and it is to Him that you belong. He gave you everything, so how can you refuse Him anything? How can I avoid His call if it is to Him that I belong! To whom do I belong? Tell me! Tell me, my brothers!"

"It is to Him that I belong!" repeated the crowd.

"Yes, my brothers, it is to Him that I belong, and it is His road that I take. He who does not take the path of God, this man, my brothers, is of incomplete faith! His faith serves him no purpose, for it is the definition of an incomplete thing! Have you ever seen a car run on three wheels? Tell me!"

Nobody had ever seen such a miracle. Heads shook in concert.

"No. We have never seen a car run on three wheels!"

"No, my brothers. A car with three wheels, an incomplete car, will not take you to your destination. The same is true of faith. If it is incomplete, it will not lead you to Paradise. Where do we want to go, my brothers, to spend eternity? Paradise or Hell? Tell me? Paradise or Hell?"

"Paradise!" thundered the crowd.

"My brothers, Glory be to God Almighty. All those who want to complete their faith and take the path of God should come see me at the end of the prayer."

# 11

At certain hours of the day, the spring turned into a full-blown cross-roads. In early morning and late afternoon, the Nawis, like the other villagers in the area, came to stock up on water. Located on a hilly spot abutting the mountain, you had to cross miles of steppe and climb over several boulders to access it. The water seeped into the rock and emerged fresh and crystal clear. Nobody knew the source of these precious drops, which didn't peter out even in dry periods, but they all knew that without this gift of nature, life wouldn't have been possible in the region.

Baya avoided the spring at peak times. She preferred to go when there were fewer people, to spare herself the routine conversations. What was she supposed to say to a cousin or neighbor who asked after her parents?

She could tell them how they were doing, then burst into tears and collapse on the ground, or lie and feel even more alone. They were old and worn down, and if growing old in comfort was unbearable, then growing old in Nawa was a real nightmare. Her father spit up blood every morning and could barely move the rest of the time. Her mother was slowly losing her sight and spent her days sidling along the walls and groping around, trying to remain active all the same, picking up anything left on the floor and in every corner as she passed. And amid this tableau, her little brothers and sisters, barefoot, crying for food.

This desolate sight weighed on her every day, and many times she hid to weep over her plight and her powerlessness. Even Toumi and his sweet words couldn't make her smile. On the contrary, she resented him for being unaware of her suffering, for being as poor as she was, and on top of everything, for not having any ambition. The romantic gestures that once amused her now annoyed her, and when he talked about marriage and children, she wanted to shake him, yelling, "Are you blind or just stupid? Don't you see that's not what I need?"

So she avoided him like she did everybody else.

That made things easier. Her decision was made and her departure imminent.


But Toumi was positioned at the spring in his new tunic, hopping with impatience. He hadn't seen her in a month! He missed her like a prisoner misses the sky. Desperate, he had decided to camp out at the water source, and finally there she was, approaching astride her mule. His heart was beating fast, and he jostled in place like a child. Since adolescence, theirs had been a platonic love story, and modesty had only ever allowed them to hold hands.

"Baya, sweet Baya," he cried in delight. "You're finally here!"

When she saw him, Baya took a step back. His intrusion upset her, and her hands, holding empty water jugs, trembled in anger. She looked him up and down, then said coldly, "Toumi, what are you doing here without your jugs?"

Head in the clouds, oblivious to her anger, he passionately replied, "I didn't come for water. I came to see you."

His attitude exasperated her even more. She turned her back on him and climbed up the rocks to the spring. He followed her. As she collected water, she asked him, without turning around, "What do you want from me, Toumi?"

She insisted on using his name, which tortured him, as he wished she would call him otherwise.

"What do you mean 'what do you want, Toumi'? I stop by your house constantly, and I don't see you. I call for you, and sometimes I even dare yell out your name, but you don't answer," he complained. "I miss you, my love!"

His lamentations didn't appear to move her. He couldn't even get her to look at him.

"You'll have to get used to it," she said. "I'm going to the capital to work. I have a cousin there who found me a job as a live-in maid."

Toumi felt the sky fall on him; he was stupefied by the news. The capital? To be a live-in maid? All live-in maids are like Baya, young girls from the country. They're hired to work in well-off suburbs to make sure the homes run smoothly: cleaning, ironing, cooking, and other tasks in exchange for a roof and wages. Though most of these girls send their pay home to help their parents, their fates all differ. Some are welcomed by families that consider them as one of their own, others by families harboring perverts. Some fall in love and get married, others get pregnant and disappear. None of that filled him with confidence. His body was heavy, including his tongue. He silently watched Baya fill her jugs and mount her mule. As she rode away, without a goodbye, he snapped out of it and caught up with her.

"Baya! Wait! I don't want you to go," he protested.

Baya stopped her mule abruptly. "You're not my father, Toumi! For that matter, do you know how he's doing? You're not my mother either, Toumi. And for that matter, do you know how she's doing? They're both sick and they're both dying. They need to go to the doctor, they need medicine. How am I going to pay for that? Huh, Toumi? Answer me!

How am I going to pay for that? Are you going to help me? So tell me, what's your plan? Are you going to pick prickly pears like your buddy Douda every time you need money?"

Toumi lowered his head. She was in as much pain as he was, but determination had stifled her feelings. She released her mule's bridle and left Toumi planted on the steppe like an alfalfa root.

# 12

"There's a smell of sulfur in the air," lamented Sidi.

The reason his neighbors' sartorial choices and new vocabulary were causing his heart such worry was because, in a past he had hidden away, he'd seen how they were used, and he knew the extent to which such accessories could allow the devil to pass for a monk. Was that devil, who had defeated him once, in Arabia, back on his doorstep?

Whereas Qafar, the little neighbor, was capable of producing gas in abundance, thanks to wind passed by its forebears, mystery still surrounded the subterfuge employed by the patriarchs of the vast kingdom of Arabia to saturate its subsoil with a black, reeking liquid, elevated to the rank of gold: oil.

King Farhoud maintained the mystery, as did many others. After being the land of poetry and then of the Revelation, Arabia became the kingdom of whispers and secrets. Accordingly, to fool his subjects about the origin of this godsend, the king delighted in telling, with more than a hint of pride, the story of his great-grandfather, the founding king who, backed by British planes, declared independence from the Ottomans, leaving nothing of their envoys in the holy lands but their red tarboosh hats. At the time, the kingdom was still just sand dunes, home to Bedouins living in destitution. The king would visit his tribes and could be very generous toward those who prostrated themselves before him. One day, he noticed an old woman in great suffering. Being charitable, as was custom, he rewarded her with a few gold coins. She then threw herself at his feet and prayed, hitting the ground with her hands.

"May the Good Lord reveal to you all His treasures!"

A few weeks later, oil was discovered. The treasure was in fact an enormous field of rank liquid.

The find occurred in the mid-1930s, and its impact on life in the kingdom was not inconsequential. With oil, this land of austere Bedouins, who considered any intrusion into their way of life as heresy, saw the arrival of people and oddities, both of which had to be approved by fatwa. Only the ulema were allowed to sweeten the pill. His Majesty Farhoud could still remember the giant refrigerator General Eatmore had gifted to the royal family. The eminent military officer had come in person from Texas to exploit the oil fields in exchange for his friendship, a few gifts, and many promises. Like most members of the court, King Farhoud, a teenager at the time, had spent entire days opening and closing the doors of the refrigerating curiosity, hoping to surprise the jinn who was hiding inside, amusing himself by turning water into ice crystals.

The kingdom transformed as the world changed and began to worship oil as a primary energy source. And even though barrels were sold cheaply to friends, the manna they brought was enough to eradicate hunger and explore the ocean depths and attain the farthest reaches of space. But it wasn't to be. The king and his descendants had lower-scale ambitions for this money. Palaces with toilets adorned with precious gems, Ferraris mounted on gold rims, private concerts with big stars, and slot machines from Las Vegas casinos.

But in order not to tarnish their reputation in the eyes of the believers, the excesses of the self-proclaimed guardians of faith were well-kept secrets. Better yet, they had achieved the feat of freezing time, throwing a medieval cloak over Arabia, allowing only a facade of modernity: television, chips, jars of mayonnaise, and so on. Women remained a vice to be hidden, and the sword and the whip were the rule. Sins have been the same since the dawn of time, so why on earth change the punishments? And so it was commonplace to whip troublemakers and chop off thieves' hands and behead heretics with a saber in the town square.

That was why the recruiter for the agricultural cooperative asked Sidi several personal questions during his job interview. It was the late 1960s, and Sidi's country, independent for a decade, was sinking into poverty following its failed experiments with socialism. As for Arabia, the kingdom was trying its hand at agriculture through a massive program that required foreign labor to be recruited left and right.

Sidi had read the job announcement in the newspaper. In the public imagination, Arabia was a land blessed by its history and its lucky star, so he decided to seize the opportunity.

The recruiter had a binder of specific instructions. The only acceptable hires were skilled male workers, visibly virile, who were deeply religious practicing Muslims. For as decreed by the famous fatwa, the Eatmores, even the beardless ones, were the only infidels authorized to work in the kingdom. And that was why the recruiter was happy to note during the interview that Sidi had a splendidly robust mustache before inquiring about his morals and competencies.

"You work with bees?"

"Yes."

"Since when?"

"Since always."

"You have hives?"

"I manage ten on behalf of the cooperative, and I have five at home."

"Interesting! Do you know how to breed queens?"

"Yes, I do."

## Anger

*Of the bear it is said that when he goes to a beehive for honey and the bees begin to sting him, he forgets about the honey and concentrates on revenge; and, because he wishes to revenge himself on all the bees that sting him, he succeeds in revenging himself upon none of them. Whereupon his anger turns into rage and he throws himself on the ground helplessly clawing the air with his paws.*

Leonardo da Vinci
*Bestiary*

# 13

Sidi worked for one of the many crown princes on a farmstead in the middle of the desert. Though the conditions were difficult and the pay disappointing, he never balked at his task. He loved his job and with his bees helped transform the farm into a small piece of heaven. Water was brought in from filtration stations, the dunes were flattened, and the ground covered with cultivable earth through which snaked the thin streams of an irrigation network. Plants flourished in the gardens, and the fields of fruit trees thrived thanks to the expertise of foreign market farmers and agronomists. During the bloom season, his girls set to work and produced a rare honey, for this was the thing about the desert—it enhanced everything, good or bad, beautiful or ugly.

Like the rest of the employees, Sidi was forever under the supervision of natives who knew nothing about agriculture. Their science was of the religious kind and they used it to settle matters, regardless of the circumstances. In this way, the farmstead director upset his agronomists' plans and decided that the fruit trees would be lined up facing southwest. Greater exposure to the sun, but little matter! Because when positioned in this way, they would be turned toward Mecca.

He silenced his objectors with forceful arguments. "Didn't Abraham turn toward God when his own people had lit a pyre and thrown him upon it? And what did God do? Did He not transform the fire into coolness and peace upon Abraham? And in the same way the trees will turn toward God, and God will transform the heat of the sun into coolness and peace upon them, and they will produce more than they have in the shade."

There was no point protesting. The foreign workers were there as underlings, a fact of which they were continually reminded, sometimes with, but often without, tact.

Sidi didn't dwell much on the local customs and enjoyed as best he could the Arabia of the poems of yore. He escaped to the desert when the opportunity arose, day or night, astride a horse or a camel. He immersed himself, body and soul, in the desert, seeking harmony in the coolness of a cave or beneath the star-filled sky. Sometimes, when he thought himself alone, a gazelle or oryx would enter his field of vision like a bolt of lightning, and sometimes, he would stumble upon ruins emerging out of nowhere, vestiges of a distant past.

But most of his time was spent working. He was constantly nurturing new hives to match the farm's expansion and satisfy the pressing demands of the court, whose honey consumption was beyond belief. So much so that he could barely keep any in reserve. At every harvest, a palace representative came to pick up the entirety of his stock, which had been carefully poured into stainless steel tanks.

After three years of unrelenting production, Sidi understood the reasons for this staggering level of consumption.

That spring, exhausted by his pilgrimage to Mecca, the prince came to the farmstead to relax.

The farm director had been informed of his arrival by phone the night before and immediately gave everyone their marching orders to welcome him properly. As some laborers mowed the lawns and cleaned the paths, others began to erect a massive tent worthy of a Mongolian emperor. In the middle of the oasis, not far from a stream, they hammered in stakes, pulled ropes, and raised the burlap structure. The interior was lined with pashmina, and the ground covered with goatskins and Persian rugs. Workers brought in comfortable chairs, sofas, and makeshift beds decorated with ostrich feathers. They hung curtains, lamps, and thin veils. Ethiopian incense was set out alongside jugs of holy water and baskets of exotic fruit. The farm was almost ready to receive its distinguished guest.

There was just the question of honey. Though the court was only passing through the farm, the director demanded a tank of five gallons.

"Five gallons?!"

"Five gallons."

The flowers had just begun to bloom, and Sidi didn't have much honey in stock. To supply this volume, he would have to steal food from his girls. Obeying this order meant starving them.

Though upset, he didn't argue. If he objected, the director, scratching at his beard and playing the religious scholar, would invariably tell him a story about the life of Noah or Jonas, or perhaps the Last Prophet, to let Sidi know that he would do well to obey. With a heavy heart, the beekeeper opened his hives and bitterly began to make the requisite, repugnant motions. He blackened his soul to meet the prince's needs.

The guest of honor arrived the next morning with his royal entourage. The laborers were told to work as usual while keeping their distance from the camp. Only Sidi was free to move about as he pleased due to the wide range of his hives. He glimpsed a modern caravan of five Hummers and heard the farm director welcoming the arrivals with the greatest possible deference. While the hired hands were unloading the cars, Sidi's keen ear detected female voices.

His worker bees had begun the day eagerly at dawn, flocking around the fruit trees at the bases of which Sidi had placed the hives. Aware of their lack of provisions, the bees were multiplying their flights at a dangerous frequency.

"Forgive me, my beauties . . . It's because the prince is here," apologized Sidi, head and voice low.

Bent over one hive, he felt a presence behind him. He turned around but the shadow had already moved. He turned again and that's when he saw her. She was across from him, amused by his gesticulations and monologue.

Sidi, thunderstruck, remained frozen like a pillar of salt.

Though a few female whispers had reached him in the wind, he hadn't imagined he'd find himself face-to-face with one of their sources, sporting a summer dress, bare feet, and untamed hair. Women in the kingdom were forced to live in silence and behind veils, for the devil inhabited their hair, their skin, and their vocal cords. They didn't have the right to venture far from their guardians, because if left to themselves, they'd be defenseless against the devil hiding between their legs. Such were the codes established by the bearded men elevated to the ranks of ulema and such were the laws of the kingdom. Breaking them could easily result in a bleeding back or a rolling head.

"Are you talking to yourself?" she asked him.

"I was talking to the bees," he mumbled.

"I'd be more reassured if you were talking to yourself," she laughed.

She was young. She must have been his age, or nearly.

"So what were you saying to them?"

"I was telling them not to worry. That all they need to do is flap their wings and they will find guidance."

The young woman's face looked sad, open but furtive.

"And they listen to you?"

"I think so."

Like a mirage, she disappeared as suddenly as she had appeared, leaving him open-mouthed, wondering whether he had dreamed her up.

He spent the night in a kind of hallucinatory fever. He was agitated, turning over and over in his bed, thinking about her . . . What was her name? Where did she come from? Was she a princess? What did he know about princesses other than that they were destined for princes?

The next day, he waited, at the same time and spot. He was losing all hope of seeing her again when she reappeared, eclipsing everything in her path. She was there, infusing the air with her scent, and once again, she smiled at him.

"How are the bees?"

"They're working," he responded idiotically, drowning in that smile.

"And you're the beekeeper?"

"Yes."

"You benefit from their work!"

"All nature benefits from their work. But I take care of them. That's my job."

"It seems like a pretty relaxing job."

"It can be dangerous."

"Oh, so what are the risks exactly? A bee sting?"

"Or a bear attack!"

She laughed. "Is that all?"

"Absolutely, ma'am!" he replied in all seriousness. "And not just any bear. A real Numidian bear, no doubt one of the last specimens."

"Miss," she happily corrected him.

"Miss," he repeated like a parrot.

She sat down on the ground and invited him to follow suit with a glance.

"A bear attack, huh? Tell me about it."

"There's a mountain near my village where the air is cool and the flowers abundant. I was in the habit of taking my hives there, as my father did before me, but neither of us had ever seen a Numidian bear around. Nor had anybody in the region. The species had been declared extinct two centuries earlier, and its existence had become a legend. But you could feel the bear's spirit deep in the forest, when all its creatures would go silent for no apparent reason. We suspected the bear was behind some odd markings: deep scratches in the tree bark, large prints in the mud . . . But no sightings. Until that summer, until the day I saw it with my own eyes. Brown, massive, built like a boulder."

"A Numidian bear?" she said, her face incredulous.

Sidi nodded in confirmation.

"After three weeks gathering pollen on the mountain, I began to pack up my things. I was pleased with the harvest. There was plenty of honey in the hives and you could smell it in every direction. I was preparing to load my cart when I saw it hurtling at me. A real Numidian bear, handsome but ferocious, eyes shining, riled up no doubt by the smell of honey engulfing the area."

Her eyes were shining too.

He continued: "My donkey took off and it took me days to find him. As for me, I immediately climbed up a tree and hung onto the first branch. I watched as the bear stood up and shook the trunk until I started to wobble. I thought to myself that I'd have liked to observe him in other circumstances, and I prayed to God that I wouldn't fall to the ground in front of him. Luckily, the bear quickly lost interest in me. He was there for the honey."

He stopped for a brief instant. She really was hanging on his every word.

"He circled the hives for a bit, and then he smashed one with his paw, sending the landing board, roof, and honeycomb frames flying. He poked his muzzle inside, oblivious to the fury he had unleashed! A swarm of bees immediately massed around his head, stinging him unrelentingly. He continued to explore his treasure as he tried to get rid of them, or put up with them, but all in vain. After a few minutes, his ears and nostrils were on fire. The stings he endured were so unbearable that he had to run away in haste, followed by the cloud of lightning bolts he had stirred up."

She laughed at his story and in a coyly accusatory tone, said, "You're making fun of me. You made it all up."

"You don't believe me?"

"The whole story is improbable!"

Sidi gathered his courage. "What's even more improbable is this lightning bolt that's struck me two days in a row in the same spot."

She blushed, lowered her head, then looked up and confessed. "That's true. Nonetheless, with all due respect to improbability, today I came on purpose."

His body swayed.

But approaching voices tore them from their romantic interlude. They were calling her.

"Asma, where are you?"

"So your name is Asma," he murmured.

She turned her head, stood up quickly, and hurriedly retreated. "Get out of here, quick! They can't see us together!"

Suddenly the voices took shape, and three men, including the farm director, swept in. Even in a polo shirt and a Bermuda hat, and not wearing the tunic of his official portrait, Sidi recognized the prince.

"Asma, come here, you wild gazelle!" he ordered as he approached. "You're not supposed to leave the tent!"

Grabbing her arm, he noticed Sidi a few feet away, frozen next to his hives.

"Who is this man?" he shouted.

The young woman blanched and the farm director was quick to answer, "Your Highness, this is our beekeeper."

"Ah, the beekeeper," said the prince, relaxing. "Well, come closer."

Sidi came closer, and the director signaled him to kneel. He felt weak and obeyed. He bent one leg, his knee grazing the ground. The prince patted him on the shoulder.

"The farm's honey is excellent."

"Thank you, Your Highness."

"Did you prepare my tank?"

"Yes, Your Highness."

"May God bless you. You're doing a great job," he said as he pulled a wad of green bills from his pocket. He slipped Sidi a few, then turned toward the girl. "Asma, straight back."

The director bent over and whispered, "You were lucky! Bring the tank to the tent by the end of the day."

Sidi stood up and watched Asma walk away, surrounded by her guards. He looked at the green bills in his clenched hand. He felt like he was holding vipers. He had never knelt before a man, and it wasn't money that would make up for it. He threw down the bills, which were swept away by the wind. But nothing would sweep away the memory of this woman, of this insult, and of what he would see that night.

# 14

At dusk, Sidi collected his hives and brought them to the honey house where they would spend the night, sheltered from the desert's nocturnal chill. They were calm and silent, while he was bubbling like a cauldron. His were not a people that knelt before princes, and yet . . .

The sun was finishing its gentle descent behind the dunes as he loaded the much-discussed tank in his utility van and headed toward the prince's tent. Asma was under there, and he yearned to see her. A yearning that could make a man lose his mind.

He parked at the entrance to the encampment. Seated around a fire, the prince and his companions were singing, beating *dafs*, and strumming *rababs*. When the guards saw him, they ran over to unload his cargo. But he held on to the tank and kept walking, warning them, "Careful. It's fragile. Tell me where to put it."

This allowed him to move past the singing men and enter the tent bathed in dim light. Behind the servant guiding him, his feet sank into Persian rugs all the way to two large marble basins. One was filled to the brim with dollars. The other was empty.

"Pour it in."

As the honey filled the empty basin, he looked around to see if he could find her. He first spotted the opened bottles, wrapped in towels and drowning in buckets of crushed ice. Despite the omnipresent scent of incense, his nose recognized the potent smell of alcohol, for all that it was banned in the kingdom. In the back, behind some thin curtains, he could make out the shadows of seated women. He recognized her voice amid different tones of laughter and the clinking of champagne glasses.

"Hurry up!" said the annoyed guard.

Sidi tilted the tank even more and the flow of honey thickened. Outside, the music's rhythm accelerated and the singing became more thunderous and vigorous. What's going on here? he wondered. Why are there massive basins of honey and dollar bills?

The last drop fell like a tear.

"Now get out of here!"

He left the tent, started the van, and drove toward the workers' residence at the other end of the farm. Even today, he still asked himself why he stopped in the middle of the oasis, why he turned around. And what his life would have been like if he had followed orders.

The night's hand had drawn its veils across the sky. He used the darkness to circumvent the guards until he reached the back of the tent, and his pocketknife to lightly pierce it. He knew that by defying the rules, he was risking his life. But an invisible force nailed him in place, keeping his eyes wide open and glued to his makeshift peephole.

The prince and his companions were reclining on sofas, hookahs smoking and glasses brimming with alcohol. The women were no longer sequestered, but front and center. Hiding neither their presence nor their bodies, they were dancing between the men and the basins. In reality, the tent was just a luxurious Middle Eastern nightclub.

Asma was one of the dancers, the most talented even. The diaphanous folds of her outfit created halos above her skin and completed her erotic metamorphosis. She was a temptress now, mastering her female prerogative to perfection. She made the curves of her breasts and the small of her back undulate before the prince, moving toward him like a sensual wave, alternately enticing and rejecting him, laughing as he took advantage of her gyrations to place a hand here, his head there.

Sidi couldn't believe it. Deep inside, while one voice was telling him to leave, another was commanding him to stay until the end, but his confused mind lacked the discernment to know which was God's voice and which was the devil's. He chose to stay.

The prince beat on the *daf* to silence the group.

"My friends, it's time for honey. The farm's honey is thick and sticks to the skin more than the soul to the body. Let's see what the girls rake in tonight!"

The prince pointed to Asma. "You're my favorite. You first!"

Asma undressed before the men. She gathered her long hair above her head, then sat in the basin of honey. She made sure her hips were drenched in the sacred liquid before rising and changing basins. Drops were still dripping down her thighs as she wriggled her behind in the pool of green bills.

Finally she stood up.

Her ass was covered in dollars.

"Now come here!" ordered the prince.

She complied. She turned around in front of him and presented her take. The prince unglued the dollars from her buttocks and counted them slowly, licking his fingers.

"Two hundred, five hundred . . . a thousand, one thousand five hundred, two thousand, and there's still more!" he exclaimed. "My friends, I think she's going to break the record!"

The guests applauded the young woman's feat as the prince continued to count. "Two thousand five hundred, nine hundred, three thousand dollars! Well done!" he cheered, slapping her ass. "Asma, you haven't wasted your evening. Next!"

The other girls followed in turn, and their commitment in the basins determined their reward. To the devil's delight, their bodies were dripping with divine honey, now perverted by men who at daybreak claimed to be working for God, in his holy lands, imposing their rhetoric and fatwas, their beards and clothing.

Sidi didn't stay until the end of the Roman orgy that followed. He returned the way he came, careful to brush away his footprints, then he slowly turned on the van and began driving back to the residence with the lights off. Behind the wheel, nausea overcame him. He stopped to throw up. He felt sickened, disgusted with himself. Disgusted for having bent a knee before such a man. Disgusted for having contributed this whole time to the success of these ceremonies, even risking his bees' lives. Disgusted for having been so naively charmed by this femme fatale.

Face drawn, he found the residence in an uproar. The transistor radio was tuned to Radio Cairo, which was broadcasting battle cries. An Egyptian coworker jumped on him. "Sadat just announced that he's ready to fight. We're going to take back Sinai! We're going to liberate Palestine! We're going to avenge our honor!"

Sidi didn't say a word. He was ready to leave too. To go far from this defiled land. Far from the Arabia of false believers and their obscene rituals. Ready to forget everything, to start over. But Palestine wouldn't be liberated, nobody's honor would be avenged, and the memory of the oasis, the prince, and Asma would haunt him forever. The following week, he made up a death in the family to get out of the kingdom. Back in Nawa, he led an ascetic life. He assembled a few hives, built a honey house, and made this his world. A member of a community, albeit of insects, but one that truly had God's blessing. Far from empty declarations and self-proclaimed guardians of faith. But not that far. Now their words were echoing in his village. Here they were at the base of his hill.

# 15

Douda, riding a mule, stopped in front of Toumi's hut.

"Toumi, come out of your shithole!"

Belly still round, Hadda had been dreaming of strawberries, and she had promised this was the last of her pregnancy whims. Seeing her show of joy at the red mullets passed off as sea bream, and her ecstasy when she tasted them grilled on the *kanoun*, Douda had prayed to the Good Lord that the rest of his path be quick and easy. But here he was being tested once again, barely a week later. How many kilos of sultans for a kilo of strawberries?

Toumi was taking his time coming out. Douda eventually got down and pushed open the door, but his friend wasn't there. Just his goats and chickens camped out inside the squalid hut. He circled around and noticed that Toumi's mule was missing too. He can't be at the spring, thought Douda. They had stocked up on water together two days earlier, and the still-full jugs were behind the door.

He stopped by the café, but Toumi wasn't there either. Nobody had seen him all day. Douda had a bad feeling and told himself he would come back later.

But later, like the next day and the next, there was no trace of Toumi, and Douda started to worry. He headed to Walou to find him, leaving no stone unturned, without success. In the mosque, at the dusk prayer, the imam again appealed to his audience to take the path of God.

Had his friend taken it? That night, on the way back from Walou, during the brief exchanges their exhaustion allowed them, Toumi had been brooding. He'd seemed affected by the voluble preacher's words.

After the prayer, Douda waited for the holy man, setting himself in his path.

"My sheik, I have a friend named Toumi. A young man in his twenties. Did he come see you about taking the path of God?"

"There are many young men who come see me about taking the path of God." The man smiled as he tried to slip by.

"He's about my height, thin, with curly hair."

The man tried again to evade him so he could greet his followers, but Douda barred the way.

"My sheik, please make an effort!" he insisted. "He left without a word. And I'm worried. So are his parents."

The imam lost patience.

"If your friend took the path of God, then may he be blessed. You should be worrying about yourself!"

"But I do my prayers every day!"

"As if that's enough!" With one motion, the imam hailed two massive men with shaggy beards for reinforcement. They crossed the room, grabbed Douda's shoulders, and unceremoniously removed the troublemaker, wriggling in their arms like a worm, from the mosque.

Night fell, men deserted the streets. Douda resigned himself to going home with no answers. On the road to Nawa, beneath an olive tree, he cried for his lifelong friend. Something deep inside told him that Toumi had left to die far from his garden.

# 16

Since discovering the villagers' odd new appearance, Sidi went down to Nawa even less often than usual. During the day, he concentrated on his new queens, and at night, he questioned whether he should leave once again, far from the tunics, beards, and veils.

But the macabre discovery of that March morning relegated his memories and unease to the background. An entire colony devastated, the honey stolen in record time. What had happened during his absence? The time it took to walk to the spring and back wouldn't have sufficed for any known predator to carry out such a destructive act.

He had spent the day examining the surrounding area but in the end didn't find a single clue. He even returned to Nawa to drink a coffee at Louz's café so he could question the villagers. Though they knew what had happened, thanks to little Béchir, they had nothing to offer but compassion. No leads or eyewitness accounts to help him solve the mystery.

All night long and into the morning hours, he mulled over the terrible scene. Thirty thousand bees ripped to pieces at the base of their hive. A massacre both large-scale and surgical that left him stunned.

To whom had death decided to allot such power?

Since he had enough water for the week, he decided to stand guard and keep his hives in sight. If this evil wrath were to strike again, he would be there to ward it off.

He observed his colonies closely, conducting patrols day and night. Alone and alert but with no idea of the kind of danger lying in wait for him.

Sometimes, overcome with exhaustion, he would doze off in his chair, but his sleep, filled with nightmares, was far from restful. He dreamed that extraordinarily hairy men wielding scissors were attacking his girls in their citadels. The bees rushed at them but were cut down midflight. Those darting in and out failed to strike their adversaries, their stingers caught in shields of hair. They were helpless before the attackers, who left no survivors—worse, they ate the larvae in the cells and drank the honey in the honeycomb.

Sidi would startle himself awake, swimming in the cold sweat of anxiety, and immediately run to his field, oil lamp in hand, to inspect his hives one by one. No extraordinarily hairy men in sight. Not yet. But he wasn't reassured. He feared the calm before the storm.

One evening, irritated by the accumulation of sleepless nights, he complained to Staka. "One week on the lookout and still nothing to report. This thing is going to fry my nerves."

His donkey, phlegmatic, sympathized.

"An evil that strikes midday doesn't need night to strike again," he seemed to suggest, before closing his eyelids and leaving Sidi to his worries.

Sidi noted how calm the animal was and agreed. "You're right. This is a daytime scourge. It's best that I sleep too before I lose my mind."

He sank into slumber and awoke refreshed.

His intuition proved correct, for that morning wasn't like any other. And yet the day began as usual: the worker bees weaving between their hives and the bushes where they got drunk off horehound, myrtle, and acacia. The beating of their wings rose to the sky in a collective prayer giving thanks to God. But a noise soon interrupted that prayer, a noise that Sidi was quick to notice.

As soon as they detected it, his girls modified their behavior. The worker bees hastily returned, and the drones began to amass on the landing pads. The bees were vibrating as one and sending each other a message. The colonies were on alert and so was he.

The humming was loud and particular, new to him.

Sidi followed the sound, and there he saw it clearly between the branches: a winged insect, large enough to be visible and audible from a few hundred feet away, though at this distance, he didn't recognize it by either its appearance or the noise it emitted in flight.

It came closer.

Now that it was less than a hundred feet away, the hives went quiet. Sidi began to make it out more clearly. Was it a hornet? he asked himself. If it was, it was the first time in his life that he had seen one this size.

The insect landed on a hive, and Sidi, who didn't let it out of his sight, ran over. It was definitely a hornet, but with atypical colors and enormous proportions. Unlike the hornets common in these parts, with their black and white stripes, this one was almost entirely black. Its funereal garb was interrupted only by an orange stain between its eyes and rings the same color that tapered across its abdomen. Its feet were hairy and its back covered with a thick layer of fuzz. And whereas a bee was as small as a fingertip, the strange visitor was as long as a finger.

"Who are you?" asked Sidi.

He knew perfectly well that the insect wasn't going to divulge the secret of its identity. For that matter, it was ignoring him, as well as the drones ready to charge it. It strutted along the hive walls, abdomen vibrating, as it explored the terrain. Sidi was careful not to touch it, but not out of fear of its great size or its incredible menacing stinger.

He suspected the creature of being involved in the recent massacre but didn't know how. He had settled for analyzing its movements when he picked up a new, pungent smell in the air. Then the hornet flew away, and Sidi watched it disappear into the landscape.

The drones retreated a little, and the forager bees pricked the ends of their antennas outside. The worker bees got back to work, and everything returned to order. But Sidi feared the worst. The hornet's dance and the smell it had released didn't augur anything good.

# 17

Two hours later, Sidi heard them. So did his girls.

The buzzing was at fever pitch and imposed silence on the surroundings, like a bugle announcing war.

The cavalry came out of the woods. This time, Sidi didn't need to squint and look around for the source of these wrong notes. A horde of giant hornets surged from the trees, cloaked in black, broadcasting their murderous intentions in broad daylight. They were twenty or so in total. There was no longer any doubt—these were the culprits.

The colonies quickly moved into a defense configuration. The queens returned to the sacred quarters, the foragers and worker bees sought shelter, and many of the drones stationed themselves on the landing pads while the rest flew in front of the hives, forming a first shield. But the cloud of hornets headed in the direction of one hive in particular: the one on which the first hornet had performed its solitary dance and dispersed its scent.

Sidi rushed to his shed. He had recognized the strategy. They were plunderers and the first hornet had merely been a scout. It had left its nest in search of a citadel to pillage. The hunt successful, the scout had marked the target with its pheromones. This allowed the hornet to find the hive again, leading a horde of its kin looking to sack, kill, and steal before heading back into the brush.

"Not this time!" Sidi raged. In front of the hut, Staka was agitated, braying as loudly as he could. The elders say that a donkey brays when the devil appears, and his master didn't disagree.

"You see them too, do you?"

Inside, Sidi rummaged through his scant belongings for a jar and his old beekeeper suit, inherited from his father. In harmony with his girls, he hadn't worn it in decades. They recognized him and didn't defend themselves when he raised the roof of their house for one reason or another. But now, he couldn't risk confronting these gigantic insects without precautions. Plus, hornets sting at will, unlike honeybees, which, as soon as they sting you, lose their stingers and their lives. If this squadron turned against him, without a suit, he'd be in trouble.

He returned to the hives at a run. The attack was imminent.

The giant hornets hovered across from the marked hive. Given how few the attackers were, the citadel appeared impregnable. Indeed, an army of small soldiers had formed at the entrance, all possessed by the same vibrating, humming waves, as if inciting each other to battle. Above them, the cloud of drones was massing in the air to block the hornets' passage. These bees, whose lives were often reduced to fertilizing the queen, were finally going to distinguish themselves in a true face-off.

But the assailants didn't seem to fear these intimidation maneuvers. They were certain of their superiority in the barbarian art of war and knew that this tribe was no match for them. After observing for a few minutes, the hornets abruptly went on the offensive. They rushed the drones like seagulls on a school of sardines, hunting them one by one. After catching them between their hairy feet, they ripped them in half with a jerk of their jaws, or ran them through with a jerk of their stingers. The bombardment was constant and at high frequency. The bodies piled up at incredible speed, whole or in pieces, and began to form a small heap below the citadel. Most of the warriors died immediately and fell as motionless as autumn leaves. The others, gravely injured, twirled in the air before dying amid the corpses.

Three thousand drones fell for the glory of the colony. It took the giant hornets only half an hour to destroy the first shield.

They neared the landing pad, the only way inside, and began touch-down maneuvers. The bees no longer dared fly. They were posted at the entrance, stressed and nervous, still vibrating en masse, forming a hesitant and disintegrating swarm as they waited for hand-to-hand combat on the ground.

Hairy feet touched the hive walls, and the death squadron surrounded the opening. Moving slowly and confidently, its members advanced together, orange marks on their foreheads, preceded by immense antennas guiding them on the path to treasure. Once they reached the edge of the pollen trap in which Sidi's girls were shivering, ready for sacrifice, the gruesome operation resumed. Being outnumbered didn't scare the hornets, nor did their dwindling swarm. They swooped on the honeybees, delivering violent and fatal blows.

The bees flowed out of the trap and tried to block the raiders, but they were helpless against the untiring, terrifying jaws into which they hurled themselves by turns. In rapid-fire offensives, the bees were harpooned and promptly ripped apart by the pitiless predators. Their tiny stingers and little teeth were up against dense coats of hair and armored shells. And even, on several occasions, when they tried to attack simultaneously, two or three against one hornet, their target didn't appear to feel the sting. Benefiting from greater size and strength, the hornet easily thwarted its adversaries' tactics. Kicking the bee aiming for its abdomen while striking another with its stinger, the hornet would take on yet another attacker coming straight at its enormous head, and then twist to send the final foe, going for its wings, spinning away.

After a few minutes, the squadron of black hornets had decimated a thousand worker and forager bees. The barrier built with their bodies to protect the sacred quarters broke apart entirely before the incessant bombardment. Soon the landing pad would give way and the colony would fall.

During this time, head in his helmet, Sidi had been observing the scene in silence. His mind was focused, his soul devastated. It was time to intervene.

"So that's how you did it. Well, this time, you won't finish the job," he said.

He knelt at the hive entrance, as if in prayer, and crushed a hornet that was sawing at the entrails of one of his girls. Striking hard, Sidi felt its hard shell yield under the impact of his fist. Its stinger emerged from its abdomen like a spear and stuck on his glove. Its jaws continued to move and were still clicking when he tossed it to the ground, dead.

In their murderous frenzy, the other hornets hadn't stopped the attack. This allowed Sidi to kill five more before they became aware of his irksome presence. They immediately changed strategy. They took off from the launch pad and turned their attention to Sidi.

Sidi knew it was pointless to flee—the aggressors would pursue him. Though he threatened them with large motions, killing a few more in the process, they refused to retreat. He would have to wipe them out to the last one, for it was in their instinct to exterminate anything that came between them and their spoils, even if it cost them their lives.

The battle raged. The hornets harried and charged him from every direction. Some tried to slip through the folds of his suit to reach his flesh, others violently flung themselves against his helmet, and he saw their eyes up close—red, as if injected with blood. Their stingers pierced the stitches of his garment and the veil of his helmet, narrowly missing him. But Sidi had always been incredibly dexterous. He was the son of the mountains and the hills, accustomed to its animals and insects. His mind and movements were still sharp, protected from the weight of his years by the nectar produced by his girls. They were watching over him the same way he watched over them.

Through a surprising choreography of delicate sidesteps, powerful blows, and a few twirls, he crushed the furious invaders one by one between his gloves and placed the last one in the jar alive. He then hurriedly cleaned the battlefield and buried the thousands of corpses lying on the ground. He rubbed the hive walls with a rag soaked in jasmine water to expel the gruesome smell. He opened the roof, and light flooded the inside of the citadel. The honeycomb frames were gleaming like slabs of gold. The brood was as warm as a maternal belly, full of thriving larvae, unaware of the battle that had just been waged. The queen was still hiding in her quarters, surrounded by traumatized, disoriented bees. But it didn't take long before life and breath prevailed over fear and terror. The queen eventually emerged and comforted the kingdom with her scent, the worker bees got back to work, and the drones resumed flight.

# 18

Sidi placed his head next to the jar.

Since its capture, the black hornet hadn't stopped flying, banging body and stinger against the glass walls.

"What aggressiveness!" marveled Sidi.

Even though he had found those responsible, he didn't know anything about them.

He had observed their bodies of exaggerated proportions, their reconnaissance technique, and their attack plan. None of it was familiar to him.

He knew the local flora and fauna, and yet he had never seen this species before. Hornets this size couldn't have been lying in wait all these years and, as a queen breeder, he knew that evolution was a slow and tortuous process. Nature couldn't have birthed such a monster overnight. This hornet undoubtedly came from somewhere else. It had traveled.

Sidi had been equally attentive to the behavior of his bees toward the aggressors, and he had quickly understood that they were completely vulnerable to this unprecedented menace.

He thought back to the scene of destruction and the bravery of the drone bees.

Normally, the drones served only one purpose to the hive. Their essential mission was to fertilize the queen during her nuptial flight, and as soon as the empress was satisfied, the worker bees unceremoniously chased the drones out of the kingdom, letting them die of cold and hunger. A sad fate, he had often thought, when he collected their dead bodies at the end of summer.

On the other hand, in the event of an attack, the drone bees formed the first line of defense for the citadel.

Since the new queens he'd introduced had been impregnated, he knew that the worker bees were already planning to expel the drones. In a way, they were already doomed.

By letting them confront the hornets, he had offered them the chance to distinguish themselves on the field of honor without endangering the colony's survival, and in the process given himself the chance to note with his own eyes the nature and actions of these barbarian insects.

But the drones had been powerless before the black hornets.

He'd also wanted to see how the other bees would react to the attacks. They were crazed, and yet, they didn't retreat. Their desperate counterattacks, as individuals or in tiny groups, had had zero effect. They didn't know how to defend themselves from these monsters, he had noted before ending the massacre.


"Where are you from? How did you get all the way here?" he murmured to the hornet thrashing around the jar.

The day had ended without further conflict, and when he saw evening come and his girls return to their hives as usual, he felt reassured. The hornets were in fact diurnal insects, and, until tomorrow at least, he would be granted a truce. He needed to use this time to his advantage. He needed to think. He set his mind to work, pacing in his hut, at times scratching his head, at others pulling on his mustache, turning in circles like the hornet in the jar, colliding against the invisible walls of his ignorance, until he collapsed in exhaustion alongside his tireless guest, still trying to pierce its glass trap.

"You want to get back to your people, don't you?" he asked.

Hearing his own words, the image of his people, the Nawis, decked out in their new getups, leaped into his mind and he had a realization. This hornet wasn't the product of natural evolution; it was a sign of nature, derailed.

This imbalance in the ecosystem bears the mark of man, concluded Sidi.

He wrapped the jar in a piece of cloth, placed it under his arm, and untied his donkey.

"Let's get a move on, Staka."

The donkey galloped all the way to the central square where the villagers killed time with rounds of scopa and hookahs. Once again, his presence prompted enthusiasm and his countenance concern.

"Come sit down!" one Nawi said.

"Everything okay?" asked another.

Seeing him in his white garb was a first for them. Caught up by the day's events, he had forgotten to change and had removed only his helmet. His weary face bore the marks of his recent sleepless nights and the monstrous battle waged a few hours earlier.

"What are you waiting for, Louz? A Turkish coffee, please!" he said.

The server responded in a lilting voice, "Right away, with a touch of rose water. I'm pouring it myself. But don't say anything until I'm done."

Men gathered around Sidi to hear his news. Once they were all situated, he took out the jar and set it on the table. Seeing the gigantic insect, jaws clacking like reapers, aggressiveness seeping from its glass prison, the Nawis took a step back.

"Good lord!"

"What is that thing?!"

"I captured this in my field this morning and wanted to know if I'm the first person in the village to see one."

"You ever see that before?" one villager asked another.

"No!"

"And you?"

"And you?"

"And you?"

Heads shook in unison, lips flapped . . . Nobody had ever come across such a creature. The crowd sent up a rumbling of "nos" before being cut off.

"I've seen one before!"

Everyone turned toward the voice coming from the back. It was Douda. He looked embarrassed, and dark rings dug into his cheeks. He had been mulling over Toumi's disappearance for several days, but the sight of the giant hornet snapped him out of his thoughts.

Five months earlier, at the giveaway extravaganza led by the bearded men, Douda had grabbed more stuff than anyone. Energized by his wife's pregnancy, he had made several round trips and each time went home loaded like a camel. When it came time to unpack, he began with a crate of blankets. "It must have been this big," he said, miming a box about three square feet. "It wasn't completely full. There was something else in it. A cardboard sphere clinging to a corner."

"A cardboard sphere?"

Douda swallowed and continued. "Yes, big as a melon. I shook it to see what it was, and a dozen insects like that one immediately came out. I was so surprised that I fell backward, but they didn't attack me. They flew out the window right away."

"Do you still have the crate?"

"Yes, behind my place."

Douda led Sidi, and the village followed behind. With the help of an oil lamp, Sidi examined the crate and then the ball the size of a small melon. It was made of a strange material, like heavy-duty paper, and its walls were irregular, solid, and completely opaque. There was a hole in it.

Before the villagers' curious gaze, he cut it in half. What he saw turned his blood to ice. A hexagonal grid of dark cells filled the sphere. Inside those cells were dead larvae and a few black hornet cadavers, withered but no less terrifying. This necropolis was a nest, a swarm of black hornets . . .

They were here.

# 19

As he returned to his hut, Sidi was immersed in thought. He gathered the elements, situated the facts, allowing his intuitive imagination to fill in the holes.

Staka advanced slowly, as if joining in his master's deep reflection.

The story must have begun in a warehouse, in another country, or even on another continent. A black hornet queen, sensing the warmth of wood, had settled into a crate of merchandise and made her nest. Bad luck. No sooner had she finished and laid her first eggs than the crate was moved and packaged for a long trip, most likely at the bottom of a shipping container, in the hold of a plane or boat, with other crates and other cartons. The cargo crossed miles before reaching the bearded men, who generously distributed it in Nawa, slipping Pandora's box to the unlucky Douda. The queen and the few members of her fragile court that had survived the journey were waiting for the moment they could escape their suffocating trap. So when Douda opened the crate and shook the nest, they took off and vanished into the wild. The region's gentle climate agreed with them. The queen created a new swarm, and her nest survived the winter.

Where had the bearded men gotten their goods?

Sidi had inspected the crate from every angle, and the other crates too, in search of clues, but there was nothing written on them. The clothes and blankets didn't have any labels either.

How could he have known?

Known that the warehouse he was imagining was part of a factory located in the province of Shaanxi in central China, giant hornet territory, and that the workers of all ages exploited there fashioned all manner of textiles, day and night.

Known that these goods had been ordered by the crown prince of the kingdom of Qafar, and that the container of hornets had traveled in the hold of his yacht.

Known that a few months earlier, the Sheik, head of the Party of God, had rolled out the red carpet at the Sidi Bou port to this same prince, bearing money and hornets, to get his party elected to lead the country.

Once again, man, in search of land, gave the plague to his fellow man in the folds of his offerings.

Back home, Sidi set the jar on the table, sat on a corner of his bed, and took off his shoes. The hornet appeared exhausted as well, and though still clicking its jaws, it had stopped flying and was now merely climbing along the glass walls. Sidi removed his white suit and put it away next to his helmet, but flashbacks of the battle were not so easily cast aside. The horde had identified him, surrounded him in a cloud, and attacked relentlessly and in unison. Even though they had only numbered twenty, the violence of their attack was such that he could have been stung a good hundred times in just a few minutes.

What would have happened to him if he hadn't protected himself with his suit before confronting them? He'd be dead, no doubt.

Before blowing out the wick of his lamp and going to bed, Sidi took another look at his new adversary and couldn't help but admire the perfection and beauty of its mechanics, all while racked by the idea of having to face it in merciless combat.

"Glory to God," he murmured. How do you confront such a beast?

Exhausted, he sank into the world of dreams.


"Read!"

Sidi started in his bed, awakened by the sound of his own voice. This word was still echoing in his head, delivered in a dream in which he'd found himself part of a trio moving between rows of books.

"Read"—the first heavenly word, the first commandment, and the key to all things. What other way to solve the enigma of the hornet than to read what had been written about it? This was the path. He needed to embark on a quest for the knowledge he lacked.

The first rays of dawn spread daylight through the dying obscurity and brought an end to the ceasefire. Soon life would resume at full throttle, and Lord help he who kept his eyes closed and limbs stiff. Sidi's mind cleared as he stretched in his bed. He washed up, prayed, and thanked God for his inspiration because even though the word *read* hadn't revealed any mysteries, it had set him on the path.

If the company of men could bring about doubt in God and the meaning of His designs, the company of bees led Sidi to quite different conclusions. He floated with them in a world of petals and pollen, of rapture and labor, rejoicing in an existence united by the elements, given rhythm by the seasons, laced with rewards. He venerated the God of his bees, unknown to many humans. He admired the beauty and precision of His work in the most concrete way possible and had made himself a place in an ancient wheel moved by divine inspiration. But now man's ambition had placed his girls in danger. This time, he was determined to protect that which was dear to him.

Light flooded the valleys, and the mountain flattened the horizon with its splendor. Sidi was already on the lookout, monitoring his colonies, preparing for an eventual confrontation. From time to time, he would warily scan the landscape. He was nearly certain that the monsters were hiding in the brush. There was no better base in the area. The steppe was inhospitable, and if they had been in the nearby hills, he would have flushed them out ages ago.

He felt torn because while he needed to read to learn, there were no books in either Nawa or Walou, apart from copies of the Holy Book in the mosques and textbooks in the children's threadbare schoolbags. Around here, you had a greater chance of coming across a five-footed sheep or a seven-headed snake than a local library or a bookstore that, on top of everything, had any encyclopedias on its shelves. If he hoped for an answer, he would have to go to the capital, and that meant abandoning his girls in the meantime. They would be alone, left to their own devices, at the mercy of a new attack. It was unthinkable.

But he hadn't counted on the mercy of God. Midmorning, as he was keeping guard, waiting for the worst, a dozen shadows appeared against the light. He made them out one by one as they mounted his hill and headed toward him. Men and women, all from the village, costumes gone, wearing their old clothes, led by Kheira. Once she reached him, she tearfully expressed everything she was feeling.

"I know that they're your girls, but they're mine too! Only God knows how much I'm hurting for them. And to think how we jumped on those damn crates! We're not going to let you confront those creatures all alone. You remember the state you were in yesterday. If the hornets come back, we'll chase them away with you!"

# BUREAUCRACY

# 20

Sidi wasn't used to outsourcing his business and even less so to asking for or receiving help, preferring to reduce his interactions with other humans to the bare minimum. But the fact of the matter was that he needed to accept this Nawi hand proffered with the noblest of intentions. He couldn't get through this without them, nor they without him. The hornets were everybody's business. If this species proliferated, the next generation of bees would serve as hornet food. The taste of honey would become a mere memory that the Nawis would conceal from their children, ashamed of their inability to preserve the marvels of this world for them.

"Come on, Kheira, dry your tears. Your timing couldn't be better— I need your help."

Then he explained his strategy to the small group. "Most importantly, cover yourselves. No skin showing!" For while his bees were gentle, the black hornets were of a rare violence, and if they took chase after a man, it would be to the death. The youngest villagers were to go tracking in the surrounding hills. And no intervention before his return, if ever the nest was discovered. The others would closely guard the colonies. One guard per hive, with instructions to unceremoniously crush the hornet scouts. In the event of a mass attack, all the guards would unite to collectively defend the targeted hive.

And he would set out in search of a book.

"Go, don't worry. I'll wait for the beasts to show up—no matter what!" promised Kheira.

He trusted them. The Nawis were hardened folk. If they encountered the hostile insects, they'd know how to keep a cool head and nimbly defend themselves.

"If I don't end up returning tonight—"

She cut him off. "We'll keep watch until you come back."


Sidi placed the jar and the little money he had in a canvas bag and headed for Walou. At the bus station, he climbed into a shared taxi going to the capital. They were seven in the van, including the driver, who looked to be entering his thirties, as did his vehicle. He had carefully placed stickers with prayers and invocations on the back windshield: *We will reach our destination if God wills it, Our lives are in your hands, my Lord,* and other declarations that preemptively exonerated him from all responsibility in the event of an accident, and even granted him road privileges. And so he drove like a stunt driver, blindly passing other cars with barely an inch to spare, stressing some of the passengers and waking others from their naps, with the help of the national radio station blasting from old speakers. After the revolution, the time had come for democracy and journalism, but what came was an endless media debate in which politicians blamed one another for all that ailed the country. That day's debate was particularly tense, for good reason—the topic was the murder of a lawyer by the name of Nazih, an emblematic figure of the left-wing party. He had been shot dead one week earlier in his car, outside his home. The perpetrators, two unidentified individuals on scooters, were still at large.

"You killed him!" A guest from the opposition was losing his temper on air. "You're allowing violence to thrive. Your radical imams are calling for murder in their sermons on a daily basis. They even have a list of people they've condemned! It's you who murdered the martyr Nazih!"

"These are serious and baseless accusations, which will be the object of a complaint of defamation filed in court. The Party of God has nothing to do with this unpleasant incident to which Mr. Nazih fell victim. On the contrary, we deplore it."

The debate spread to the taxi, also divided.

"May he rest in peace," said one passenger, a veiled grandmother.

"How can you say that?" retorted her neighbor, a bearded young man accompanied by his teacher. "He was a communist and a snob who didn't believe in God. Serves him right!"

"How do you know he didn't believe in God, huh? You could read his mind, is that it?" rebelliously interjected a younger passenger in the back seat, who had left her hair exposed.

The teacher flew to his disciple's rescue:

"No need to read his mind! His mouth was plenty big and he said what he thought loud and clear. He claimed that the law of God couldn't govern our society, that the two were incompatible. How could he voice such heresy? What does it mean, then, to believe in God? Is it just a hobby? He was a drinker and a blasphemer!"

In the back of the van, next to Sidi, was seated a giant of a man in a baseball cap, his face scarred. Hearing them, he opened the bag at his feet and took out a beer that he uncapped with one flick of his nail. He addressed the two believers: "You two! A pair of rats who've been hiding out a long time. Come and kill me if you have the balls!"

Then he tossed out a "God is great" and in one swig, downed his beer, concluding with an impressive belch.

"Calm down, please," demanded the driver. "You can have at one another, but not right now. Not in my van."

The capital was only a two-and-a-half-hour drive away, and yet it seemed like a different world, its urban frenzy a strong contrast to the stripped-down countryside. It had been a long time since Sidi had set foot here.

The driver dropped off the passengers at the train station, and everyone went their own way. Sidi dove into the streets in search of a bookstore.

In his distant memories, the city had been a magical place. The hill of the saint whose mausoleum overlooked a peaceful cemetery where white tombs were scattered in the grass like sugar cubes; the souks of the old medina that pulsated like a heart oxygenated by master artisans; the cafés in the Frankish quarter on the outskirts of town, which, early in the morning, exuded the smell of strong espresso, with the warm voice of Oum Kulthoum lending its rhythm to the hand brooms sweeping the sidewalk; the bus station, its blooming gardens, its bus and tramway lines bordered by newspaper stands and shoe polishers. These were the images Sidi had kept of the time when, as a younger man, he would come to the capital to sell a few jars of his honey.

But he didn't recognize this sad and filthy city. People were walking around with long faces, as if hungover. The public squares were surrounded with barbed wire, and the army tanks parked here and there made the whole thing even more troubling. Graffiti and various slogans decorated the walls and facades:

LONG LIVE THE REVOLUTION!
FREEDOM TO THE PEOPLE!
MAY GOD'S KINGDOM COME!
MAY GOD DAMN HE WHO PISSES AGAINST THIS WALL AS WELL AS
ALL HIS DESCENDANTS!

Trash cans were overflowing, fighting with people for space on the sidewalks. But his gaze, increasingly distressed, wasn't just focused on the litter. The strange trend that had struck his village was present here, as well. There were many women covered up in black and as many men in tunics. Had they also been given the crates? Had they also voted for the Party of God? Did they know to what danger they were exposing themselves? worried Sidi. Did they know about the hornets?

He went to the Rue des Libraires, in the south of the city, but since his last visit, the street had changed. There were no more bookstores. At best, he came upon a few stationery shops that only sold blank paper and textbooks.

He had no bearings left. He felt lost and almost got himself mowed down. Running stop signs and red lights were among the freedoms the revolution had given the people.

He took refuge in the pedestrian alleyways of the medina and headed toward its main pathway. Even if artisan crafts were quietly dying out, the old quarter was always crowded, always vibrant, mysterious. You could still discover works of art and craftsmen with golden hands. He navigated through the spices and flower essences, weaving between mosaics and *margoum* rugs. The stroll perked him up.

Sidi explored the wide avenue and its adjacent paths for two hours, and not a bookstore in sight. Just packed cafés and snack bars that never emptied, stands and stalls of various goods, from underwear to smartphones. He took a break with Ibn Khaldun, in the square named after him. This local figure was celebrated by a majestic statue depicting him reading a book, a symbol of his prolific works and his knowledge, which nobody knew anymore, or hardly. His name had become a meeting place. Before the indifference of the people skirting by him, taking him for a bum, Sidi stared at the statue in admiration and without breaking his gaze, sat on a nearby bench, as if hypnotized.

This statue of a world-weary Ibn Khaldun was the only creature around with a book in its hands. In his time, the renowned sociologist, father of the discipline, had said: "Man is social by nature."

Sidi sighed. "Face facts. You still need other people."

# 21

Despite the steam on her glasses, it took her just one try to fish her granddaughter's bottle out of the pot in which she was sterilizing it. She was simultaneously listening to the radio and thinking about a thousand different things. Both a devoted mother and an enthusiastic young grandmother, she had plenty to think about. But her usual thoughts were crowded by new preoccupations, a citizen's preoccupations. What future was in store for the country? What future was in store for her children and grandchildren in this new order?

The prime minister was speaking on the radio, trying to reassure listeners about the state of the country despite the recent urban clashes targeting the American embassy and the assassination of the lawyer Nazih. She didn't believe a word of his supposed sincerity and held the government responsible not for the country's inherited poverty but for its divisions and uncustomary violence.

Of course, she had faith, to the extent that she made sure to do her daily prayers and was planning a pilgrimage to Mecca, but she didn't look favorably on the Party of God's ascent to power. On the contrary, its legions and speeches made her hair stand on end. She felt like they were worshipping a God of hate and punishment, while hers was one of love and mercy.

The minister's spiel didn't calm her anxiety, and she eventually turned it off. Before, in the time of the Handsome One, there hadn't been news on the radio. Every song in the repertoire was already known. Then came the day when good news rang out, followed by bad news that kept coming, picking away at morale and shoving aside budding hope. Hope for a better life.

Like most of her fellow citizens, she had been euphoric when the revolution erupted, happy to see, in her lifetime, an end to the farce led by the Handsome One, who had insulted his people on a daily basis. Despite the difficult weeks that followed his flight, punctuated by demonstrations, discord, and curfews, enthusiasm didn't wane. The first free elections in the country's history were in sight. How proud they had been!

But the mountain gave birth to a mouse—a bearded mouse!—and the Party of God rose to power.

The religious competencies of its ministers didn't solve a single economic or social problem, and in many respects, the situation worsened. The country remained mired in poverty and its young people in unemployment, while the violence of a fringe of radicals and their hate-filled discourse proliferated with the leaders' complacency. Within the dream of prosperity and tolerance, nothing remained of fragile democracy but the illusory right to talk shit.

She didn't swear but she was waiting for the next elections impatiently. She was anxious, like many, to return to the ballot box and chase this ideological intrusion and its representatives out of the country. Until then, Lord help her!

The ringing at the front door interrupted her thoughts, and before it could interrupt her napping granddaughter, she ran to open the gate at the end of her small garden. Instead of the neighbor she had expected, she found Sidi.

"What a lovely surprise!" she cried, taking him in her arms.

As soon as he saw her, Sidi felt relieved. She was still the same, face beaming with light.

"Jannet! I need you."

In a country of taboos and traditions, Jannet was the only product of a marriage between villagers that ended very early in divorce. In other words, she was orphaned when she was just a baby in her crib. Her parents abandoned her to her fate, and the little girl survived by hiding in the shadows, living with relatives, at the mercy of anyone interested in bothering about her.

Tossed from one family to another throughout her childhood, she miraculously avoided the illnesses and fevers of infancy but grew up in sadness. Treated as a bastard, she was constantly subjected to drudgery and reprimands. At night, when she prayed in secret, fists clenched, she often ended up crying. All she wanted was to be loved, but all she found was the cruelty of grown-ups and of the children who followed their example. And yet the ugly duckling transformed into a marvelous human being under the noses of those who had wanted to bury her.

This emancipation never would have occurred without the aid of a distant uncle, a beekeeper who lived alone with his bees and who had taken pity on her. He couldn't do much for her, but the little he could, he did. With the firmness of solitary men, he demanded that her guardians send her to school as the law dictated. For although the Old One who had taken the reins of the country at independence had ended up mad, he hadn't been for his entire life. Every now and then, he had even been capable of flashes of brilliance.

When he was still of sound mind, he made school obligatory for all the children in the country. Instead of a saint to worship, he offered them the chance to take their fate into their own hands.

Jannet's guardians begrudgingly enrolled her in school, where the child's daily woes evaporated. School was her oxygen, the place where she was free, where she blossomed. At the first glimmers of dawn, she would walk ten miles across the steppe to sit on her school bench. She loved to learn and gave her teachers the utmost attention, finally tasting the joys of praise and honors.

But more than anything, she loved to write, because when she wrote, she felt like she existed.

The merit-based system rewarded this brilliant student, and she was granted a boarder's spot at the Montfleury High School for Young Girls, on the hill near the capital's Frankish quarter. She pursued her secondary education there, and the little girl in rags became a sublime young woman who could perfectly wield both the Arabic of Al-Mutanabbi and the French of Baudelaire.

She dreamed of becoming a teacher so she could save children on the path to perdition. This came easily to her.

She dreamed of love, and love came to her in the form of a young penniless academic.

Emerging victorious from this difficult stage of life, she didn't harbor any rancor toward her family and the past. If she had made it here, it was thanks to these people as well, including her parents.

She married and had children. She gave all the love and attention that she had been sorely deprived to her family and her students. Everywhere she went, she was sympathetic to anyone in pain, trying her best to offer support and comfort.

Years passed between two temples, home and school, worker bee and queen, bags of groceries in one hand, and in the other stacks of notebooks belonging to young minds who had written the day's date and were waiting for corrections.


Sidi looked into the crib where the baby girl was sleeping peacefully and didn't move for several minutes. He placed his finger in the palm of her hand. She squeezed it. He smiled.

"The new generation is here."

Jannet nodded in agreement.

"How old is she?"

"Fifteen months."

"*Mashallah!* What's her name?"

"Farah."

He leaned over and whispered a few words, their secrets known to him alone, then said, "May she be blessed."

In the living room, Jannet served him tea and he served up his story.

He explained the reason for his trek. Described his discovery of the initial massacre, the epic battle he had waged against the hornets, how questioning the villagers led to the original nest, his hopeless attempts to find an encyclopedia in the capital, his decision to call on her for help.

She was completely absorbed in his account, her face reacting to every detail, and when Sidi revealed the massive creature, now lying dead in the jar, she jumped back. His worry infected her immediately.

"I've never seen this kind of bug either, not in nature, or in a book. Let's talk to Tahar at the university. He has access to a well-stocked library. We're sure to find an encyclopedia that lists it."

Jannet asked her neighbor to watch her granddaughter until she returned, and then called her husband to let him know they were coming. She and Sidi climbed into a taxi together, heading for the College of Arts and Sciences.

# 22

Tahar was waiting for them in the dean's office, his office, engrossed in his newspaper. The first in a stack representing the various movements and leanings popping up right and left.

He had stopped reading the newspaper years ago, but the revolution had disrupted everything in the country, from individual to insect. In its wake, the newly won freedom of speech had given back to the press its long eclipsed credibility. Ever since, Tahar stopped at the newsstand every morning.

For nearly thirty years, journalists had updated only the slim sports and culture sections. When it came to politics, the Handsome One, as soon as he took power, would prepare them the pot of daily soup to be served to the people.

And so the front pages were entirely dedicated to him. You could read that he had presided over this or that council of ministers, or that he had been honored by some university in France or Canada, or that with his blessing, Ramadan would start on such and such date. And between the lines, nothing.

Deeper in, sports journalists would enthuse over some sad little soccer championship, the new opiate of the masses, and their colleagues on the culture pages, confronted with mediocre productions, would rack their brains to fill their columns, taking a few risks even. "Hollywood to make an epic about Hannibal, our Carthaginian hero," one proudly wrote. Whereas in reality, the biopic in question was about Hannibal Lecter, the psychopathic cannibal.

When there was a scientific article, you had to buckle up. Readers learned, for example, about the successful outcome of the unexpected cross-breeding of a cowboy and his mare in California, leading to the birth of the first horse with a man's head in modern history, and about paleontologists' discovery of a one-hundred-foot skeleton in West Africa, undoubtedly belonging to Adam. Curiously, Eve's skeleton was missing. The final pages were a dumping ground. Next to a coquettish photo of an Egyptian actress or Lebanese singer would be a hadith saying not to look. Psychics and amateur psychiatrists competed for headlines with reader mail, letter upon letter confessing "I have nothing . . ." or "I've loved in silence . . ."

For a long time the country had nothing, and loved in silence.

Then, as if by magic, the Handsome One disappeared. The regime of silence had ended.

What did the people have today?

Who would they declare their love to now?

The recently launched newspapers tried to provide the answer.

"We have debts," wrote one journalist.

"Saïda Manoubia mausoleum set ablaze," wrote another. "On Tuesday night, two individuals threw Molotov cocktails at the mausoleum before fleeing," he reported, noting that this wasn't the first act of vandalism of this nature. "Several mausoleums have been burned down since the bearded ones took power. Should we interpret this as cause and effect?" dared the journalist. "Can we talk about night beards, who vandalize, and day beards, who govern? Is there a link between the two?" he asked.

"A link between the two? The five o'clock shadow preaching at dusk!" laughed Tahar bitterly.

How had those bastards dared profane the tomb of the saint who'd been sleeping in peace for eight centuries on Montfleury Hill? A remarkable, transgressive woman who had carved a place for herself in a society of men. Of unfailing virtue, she excelled in the field of theology and spiritual paths, supplanting the scholars of her time, writing her own incantations and teaching her own disciples, for whom she led collective prayers at the mosque.

Tahar thought of his wife. Saïda Manoubia had been an enormous source of comfort and inspiration for Jannet while a boarding student at the Montfleury High School for Young Girls. When her classmates went home during school breaks, she would visit the mausoleum, inhale the incense beneath its modest dome, and listen to old women recount episodes from the saint's exceptional life. She volunteered to welcome visitors and serve free meals, maintaining in this way the saint's memory, now up in smoke.

How would she react when she found out?

He sighed, then looked at his watch. He felt like journaling and he had a little bit of time before Jannet and Sidi arrived.

He started to write.

*Today, as I was talking to the vice-dean about the disastrous state of the college, two female students entered my office without knocking. They were wearing burkas and black gloves. I could barely make out their eyes beneath the fabric. They demanded that we end mixed-gender classes, set up a prayer room, and suspend classes during prayers.*

*The vice-dean and I exchanged alarmed looks. We had already noticed the emergence of this fundamentalist movement within the university. In fact, that was the subject of our discussion. The previous evening, several students had removed the national flag and replaced it with the black flag of a small terrorist group. This escalation was to be expected, but it's one thing to expect it, and another to confront it.*

*We told the students that we would take their demands into consideration. The vice-dean even pretended to write them down on the corner of a piece of paper. But the two young women insisted that he immediately post an announcement. So we got firmer, and the vice-dean stood up and asked them to go. They left the office in hysterics only to suddenly throw themselves down the stairs in a big clatter. As we watched in shock, they stood up somehow, though their covered bodies had no doubt been seriously bruised by the fall. Then they threatened to file a complaint for assault and battery if we refused to concede to their demands on the spot. We locked the door.*

*The university is in danger, like many places where the mind shines. Yesterday we feared amnesia and abandonment; today we dread fire and destruction. Now they're telling us how to talk and dress, but soon they'll tell us how to think. What will be on the agenda for tomorrow?*

*Since the Party of God's rise to power, pressure groups have formed under its indifferent and often complicit gaze. They're gnawing at the foundations of our culture from below. And above, a new wind is blowing, dry and arid like the desert in which it formed, carrying black*

*flags and imported ideas. These groups reject the idea of
a sovereign nation-state and attack its symbols and representatives. They extol a utopia of beards and veils, of
lash-covered backs, of cut-off hands and heads. An empire
in which every man would be mutilated, lacerated, or
amputated, for what man has not sinned?*

Light knocking at the door stirred him from his writing. He stood
up. It was Jannet and Sidi. He kissed his wife and shook her guest's
hand, then invited them to sit. He knew Sidi vaguely, the way you
know a distant relative. He knew the role he had played in his wife's
childhood and he had a distinct memory of the taste of his honey, as
the old man had continued to send them, through some cousins, jars
from each new harvest.

As Jannet told the whole story, Sidi silently nodded in agreement.
Tahar noted his features and his eyes—a distinctive combination of
humility, hope, and determination. Rare dignity too. He looked like a
knowledge seeker.

"I need your help," Sidi said, holding out the jar.

Tahar's eyes opened wide before the creature.

"I'll do my best."

# 23

The university library was losing its luster, though it was still one of the school's remaining gems. Dust covered many of its shelves, and often a visitor in search of information would feel like they were excavating a tomb. Despite this fossilized atmosphere and need for renovations, Sidi saw books glinting in the library aisles and felt as if he were beneath the vault of a starry sky, built of words, atop columns of ink and paper. Here was the divinity of man; here was his true temple.

He sensed that this was where he would find answers to his questions, and he advanced slowly and surely, following his guides to the life-sciences wing.

Perched on a stepladder, Tahar unearthed a multivolume encyclopedia that provided an inventory of the insects recorded by man. He blew on the book covers and ran his hand over them several times, as if to bring them back to life. Sidi set the jar on a table, upon which Tahar carefully lined up the volumes. The dean skimmed the foreword and found the year of publication: 1977.

"If this species is at least forty years old, we should find it listed here."

"This species is as old as the world. What's new is seeing it in Nawa."

Sidi paged through a volume, stumbling on the Latin letters that made up its lines. He set it down. He could only read Arabic, his mother tongue, but he knew that it was no longer the best steed for galloping along new paths of knowledge. Tahar noticed his disappointment and apologized profusely.

"I'm so sorry. Unfortunately, we don't have an encyclopedia in Arabic. Either written or translated. We'll look for you."

The couple split up the volumes, which were organized by world region. While Jannet flew through Europe from north to south, Tahar searched Africa and the Mediterranean Basin. And though they were in a rush, they couldn't help but marvel at the portrait of a graceful butterfly or a bumblebee that had disappeared since their childhood, expelled from nature by the urban jungle.

Pages upon pages of photos of insects, crowned by their scientific names and details about their existences, but not the slightest trace of the mysterious creature.

Could it have come from even farther away?

They opened the books for the rest of the world. Tahar swept through the Americas, and Jannet roamed East Asia. Midvoyage, she stopped at one page with a start. "Come look!"

The two men rushed over. She laid the book wide open on the table. The hornet was there, pinned down, photographed, identified, ready to confess its secrets.

"Is that really it?" Tahar asked Sidi, who was carefully examining the image.

"I think so," he answered, eyes shining in excitement.

But he still needed to be sure.

"Read!" he demanded.

Tahar translated each line aloud. He began by stating its scientific name: "'*Vespa mandarinia*.'"

He continued: "'Described for the first time in the nineteenth century by British entomologist Frederick Smith, the *Vespa mandarinia*, or the giant Asian hornet, is the largest hornet species in the world. Its nest is most often found in high branches. The size of a basketball, it is built by the queen using tree bark, which, once chewed and pasted, gives the nest the appearance of cardboard. Solid and perfectly opaque, a single opening at the lower end allows its inhabitants to come and go.'"

The image of the necropolis he had discovered at Douda's home crossed Sidi's mind.

Tahar read on: "'Adapted to tropical and temperate climates, this species occupies a large territory that stretches from east Afghanistan to southern Japan, covering India, Burma, and Thailand. In the adult stage, the giant Asian hornet can reach a length of nearly three inches. It is equipped with a quarter-inch-long stinger, with which it injects a powerful venom. The giant Asian hornet is an unrivaled hunter. Its preferred prey are bees, praying mantises, and other species of social hymenoptera, such as wasps and smaller hornets. Giant Asian hornets frequently decimate entire hives of bees during cluster attacks. After spotting and marking a hive with their pheromones, scouts, often alone, but occasionally in groups of two or three, return to their nest to seek reinforcements. Giant hornets, which measure five times the length and are twenty times the weight of a bee, can devastate a colony in a short period of time. A single hornet can kill forty bees per minute, thanks to its large jaws.'"

"*Ya Latif!*" prayed Jannet.

Sidi nodded repeatedly to confirm the descriptions and the indicated modus operandi. In all likelihood, this was the creature. Though its origin was improbable, its encroachment was very real.

Tahar resumed reading: "'When all the hive's defenses have been eliminated, the hornets feed on the honey and bring bee larvae back to their nest to feed their own larvae. The majority of bees in Asia were imported from Europe for honey production and are not equipped with natural defenses against the giant hornets. Their hives are particularly vulnerable. Only Japanese bees, the *Apis mellifera japonica*, have succeeded in developing an effective defense technique, called the ardent swarm. Refer to appendix.'"

"The ardent swarm?"

"The ardent swarm," confirmed Tahar.

Sidi wasn't missing a word.

"'The sting of a giant Asian hornet provokes intense pain in humans due to the venom delivered by the stinger. Multiple stings not treated in time can lead to respiratory problems and liver and kidney failure. Approximately forty deaths are reported each year as a result of giant hornet attacks. Though this species only targets humans when disturbed or threatened, its attacks are nonetheless violent and ferocious, as targets may be pursued for over half a mile at a speed of more than twenty-five miles per hour.' That's the end of the article."

Jannet invoked the mercy of God as Sidi finished committing all the information to memory.

"Can you read the appendix?" he asked.

Even though his bees weren't Japanese, he was curious to know.

Tahar read: "'The ardent swarm is a defense developed by the *Apis mellifera japonica* against attacks by giant hornets. When the *japonica* detect the presence of a scout intending to mark their hive, they encircle it by the hundreds; they then close in, forming a ball with their bodies, the hornet at its center. They begin to collectively vibrate, wing against wing, and bring the ball's temperature up to 113° Fahrenheit. This temperature is fatal for the giant hornet. Bees, however, can survive temperatures up to 118°. The *japonica* are the only bees known to exploit this defensive trait. Once the hornet has burned to death, the swarm dissipates. The bees clean any traces of pheromones and resume work.'"

Tahar raised his head, fascinated. The appendix included color photos and infrared images that illustrated the ardent swarm throughout the process, and the roasted hornet that resulted.

*"Sobhanou!"* cried Jannet. Glory to God!

Sidi was pensive. This ardent swarm was a marvel of nature. Here was the piece of science he'd been missing. After all these years of beekeeping, his apprenticeship wasn't over. Perhaps his girls still had some secrets to reveal to him.

# 24

At the library exit, Sidi bent over to kiss his hosts' hands in gratitude. They hurriedly stood him back up and reversed positions. His ignorance was theirs as well. Without him, they never would have known.

Outside, the sun was waning, and the shadows outnumbered the living. The country roads had been dangerous for some time now, and drivers no longer took them at night. For Jannet, it was out of the question for Sidi to return to Nawa that evening.

"You'll stay at our house. That way you can sleep on it."

She was determined not to let him confront those creatures alone.

Jannet and Tahar lived in a working-class suburb in the south of the capital. When they had bought a piece of land and built their home there, vines and olive trees had stretched as far as the horizon. But for decades, the neighborhood had been developing without any specific urbanization plan, exhausting the flora and fauna, but leaving residents the joys of flies and mosquitoes feasting in their trash cans.

And yet they far preferred their house to a fancy mansion facing the Eiffel Tower. Every stone that formed their home was soaked with their sweat.

Jannet served a light dinner. After that afternoon's discovery, no one had much of an appetite. They were seated at the table, preoccupied, aware they were up against a formidable enemy.

Eradicating this species is no mean feat. It's already established itself, Sidi thought aloud.

"Alert the authorities?" suggested Tahar without much conviction.

"The ones who can't even handle mosquitoes?" Jannet retorted. "We should, I agree, but if you think that it'll change anything . . ."

They eventually stopped talking.

Sidi was rewinding through the information from the encyclopedia. A giant hornet could kill as many as forty bees per minute. Did he have any chance of saving his girls? Wasn't it just a question of time before he saw them massacred, every last one?

Tahar and Jannet, heads lowered, stared at the vegetables on their plates. What if suddenly it was all gone? The equation was so simple that its simplicity rendered it unreal and almost unfathomable. No more bees: no more pollination. No more pollination: no more harvests. No more harvests: hello, famine. There wasn't enough in people's bellies as it was.

Jannet broke the silence. "Our bees don't know how to do this ardent thing?"

Sidi shook his head. After a beat, he added, "But they can learn."

"How's that?"

He explained: "Because they come up against so many parasites, bees develop different defense techniques. When confronted by a parasite that it's never encountered, a hive may be vulnerable. But by introducing a foreign queen, familiar with the parasite's dangers, and used to defending herself, the beekeeper assures the transmission of appropriate behavior to new generations of bees."

Jannet grasped the significance. "That's genetic transmission!"

"You mean that with Japanese queens, you'd be able to raise generations of bees capable of the ardent swarm?" asked Tahar.

Sidi nodded.

After dinner, Tahar prepared a bed for his guest and returned to the living room. He knelt before a present that had been in his home for many years—a Japanese geisha doll. She appeared even more intriguing now. He could hear Jannet talking to herself in the kitchen. He didn't know how this story would end, but he was sure of one thing: his wife wasn't going to let Sidi face this danger alone.

# 25

In the middle of the night, Tahar felt Jannet's elbow in his side.

"Tahar!"

"What?"

"I just had a dream."

"That's great. Now go to sleep," he said, turning over.

No luck, she kept going.

"Tahar! I just told you that I had a dream!"

"A good omen if God wills it," he mumbled, trying to end the conversation.

But she continued. "Yes, I think so. I saw Saïda Manoubia. She told me that the two of us were going to go to Japan, find a queen breeder, and bring that poor man back a Japanese queen."

Tahar smiled in the dark. She was starting to maneuver, making a strong argument right out the gate. A prophetic dream. Whenever she wanted to embark on a risky undertaking, she slept, woke up, and then explained to him that the saint had blessed her and recommended she do this or that. He couldn't help but tease her. He was a logical man and didn't believe in superstitions. In his mind, if these dreams were real, they were merely his wife's unconscious taking over from her conscious desires. And if they came true, it was thanks to her tenacity rather than their prophetic nature.

"Oh yeah? She told you that? It's crazy how she knows about all this."

Jannet turned on the bedside lamp, prompting his protests.

"I'm not kidding!" she insisted.

Tahar covered his eyes and asked, "And did she tell you what money we'll use to finance this fabulous voyage?"

"The money is my concern. All you have to do is come with me."

"What do you mean the money's your concern?" said Tahar, still shielding himself from the light with his hand. "Do you have any idea how much a ticket to Japan costs? You know it's the other side of the world, right?"

"I know that we know someone there, and that a trip to the other side of the world isn't any more expensive than a pilgrimage to Mecca."

Tahar dropped his hand. His eyes had gotten used to the light, and he could see Jannet's intentions more clearly as well.

"You would do that? You would do that for this man?"

"Yes, I would. I can, so I will."

Because she'd been dying to walk upon holy land, her children had gifted her the money for the trip when she'd retired. She had been planning to go this year or the next, but Mecca would wait.

"So you'll come with me?"

Seeing that her question was simple to the point of complication, Tahar opted to go back to sleep without responding.

When they woke up, Sidi was gone. He left them a note on the nightstand.

> *Dearest Jannet and Tahar,*
> *I had to leave early to return to my girls. Thank you for your invaluable help. If ever the happy opportunity arises, come visit me in Nawa and bring Farah with you. The country air will do her good. May God bless you.*

Sitting on the terrace, in front of their cups of coffee, Jannet started up again.

"You know, when I fell back asleep, after you fell back asleep . . ."

"Yes?"

"I saw Saïda Manoubia again."

"Again?!"

"Yes. She told me that I would bring a beautiful queen back from Japan and that it wasn't a big deal if you didn't go."

Tahar choked on his coffee.

"She told you all that?"

"Yes, she did!"

"You're not going to Japan because your uncle chased down a hornet!"

"My uncle didn't come down from his hill because he chased down a hornet, but because its buddies destroyed one of his hives and there's a big chance it'll happen again, to him and to other beekeepers."

"Come on! Be reasonable!"

"When I listen to my brain, it tells me to go. When I listen to my heart, it tells me to go, and when I listen to Saïda, she tells me to go."

"For pity's sake, enough with Saïda already!" he entreated her. "Do you really think that bringing back a few queens is enough to fight an invasion of an entire region, an entire country?"

"I know it won't be enough. But it'll be a start. After that they'll get it! Bees reproduce even faster than hornets. They'll be everywhere!"

"And your children? They didn't give you that chunk of money for this trip. Not to mention, they barely know your uncle."

"I'll explain it to them. And if they don't support me, well, too bad. I'll tell myself that I made a mess of bringing them up and I'll go anyway."

Wow, she's stubborn, he thought, watching her. She could wear down anyone and everyone with her relentless determination.

"What do you have to lose?" she continued. "You can't turn down an all-expenses-paid trip. Wouldn't you like to see a geisha for real?"

"I wouldn't *not* like to."

"I'll take that as a yes."

Tahar finished his coffee, then went inside to sit in his favorite spot in the living room. He stared at the geisha in her glass box for a long time. He'd already begun thinking about her, at the university library, when their quest brought them to the chapter about Japan.

The years had gone by, changing the scenery and generations around them, but the geisha was still the same: straight posture, face meticulously made up, perfectly tied red flower kimono, and an impeccable bun. Small feet in white socks, and her hands, one holding a white fan and the other extending a delicate palm, the final, graceful touch. Her aura extended beyond the panes. She might have just been a doll in a box, but there was no doubt—something in her had charmed him.

She was the sole survivor of the three burglaries they'd experienced in two years. With the revolution, the people were taking their revenge on the police in every way possible. Previously all-powerful and frequently unjust, the police had become fragile, overwhelmed by the explosion of petty crime and the emergence of small terrorist groups. It was no longer surprising to hear that individuals had burned down this police station or attacked that patrol unit. After every robbery that left their home trashed, Tahar would look at the impassive geisha and ask her in a tired voice, "Did you see those damn thieves? Won't you tell me who they were?"

He looked at her again, then stretched out his hand to open the door to her glass house. He took out a card yellowed by time. He had received the geisha by mail, in a package he had unwrapped before his children's amazed eyes. Had the robbers judged it to be of no value? Now it was more valuable to him than ever. She was more than a piece of decoration.

*Tokyo, October 1984*

*Dear Professor,*
*Allow me to offer you this geisha, guardian of the Japanese*
*tradition. I hope she'll find a place in your living room*
*and will remind you of our delightful conversations.*
*Sincerely yours,*
*Shinji Saiko*

The card included an address in Tokyo and a telephone number.

"You think that Shinji is still around and that he has the same number?"

"We're still around, and our number hasn't changed in decades."

"What if he doesn't answer?"

"We'll go anyway!"

"Can you imagine if he does answer?"

"That would be amazing!"

Jannet had never met Shinji Saiko, but she knew that he had been her husband's student. In the eighties, Tahar had given Arabic lessons at the Institute of Modern Languages for several summers in a row. At the time, the country was still known for its social harmony, relaxed lifestyle, and beaches of fine sand. Lots of foreigners visited, notably for language immersion courses, as part of international programs with students from France, Spain, Cuba, Canada, Germany, China, and Japan, among other countries. Established Arabic speakers, or hoping to become so, they all came to celebrate this fascinating language, how it sounded and how it was written. For a long time Tahar exchanged letters with many of them. At its height, this epistolary network numbered some fifty correspondents and just as many new worlds reaching him through the post. His children would expose the envelopes to a cloud of steam, carefully removing stamps to add to their collection, as he read and corrected letters from students now scattered across the world and wrote his responses in return. He had even visited some of them during private trips or conferences in Europe.

He remembered Shinji Saiko and the summer of 1984 very clearly. A multilingual translator for the press, Saiko had impressed him from the first day. Taking a long bow before Tahar, he had wanted to remove his shoes before stepping onto the classroom's sacred ground. Tahar found his attitude fascinating but asked him to keep on his loafers.

"What is Japan like, Mr. Saiko?" asked Tahar during his traditional round of the class, during which every student presented his or her country to the others.

"It's very different from here," he answered. "But our countries have something in common. Both are a delicious mix of tradition and modernity."

Tahar and Shinji often found themselves alone when class began at eight a.m. Foreign students were generally surprised by the country's lunar rhythm and nightlife, conducive to staying up until all hours: they would arrive late in the morning. One day, Shinji took advantage of the one-on-one time with his professor to tell him a story.

In the seventeenth century, in the city of Kushiro on the island of Hokkaido, two samurais on leave ran into each other during the spring festival. They were old friends who had lost touch because they served different masters and were both overjoyed at their reunion. They enjoyed the celebration together, having such a grand time that they promised each other they would return on the same occasion the following year. When spring came, one of the samurais, unable to make the trip in time, unsheathed his katana and performed hara-kiri. His ghost appeared to his friend in the city of Kushiro during the festivities, thereby honoring his promise.

"My friend, if everyone who was late in this country did hara-kiri, there wouldn't be anybody left. There would just be ghosts wandering through the cities," laughed Tahar, and his student with him.

At the end of the course, Shinji went back to Tokyo. They wrote each other for a while, exchanging best wishes, a few gifts. But as the years went by, the relationship, like Tahar's other correspondences, faded.

"Call him, and you'll see soon enough!"

At noon local time, six p.m. Tokyo time, as Tahar was dialing Shinji Saiko's number, his two female students, bearing medical certificates describing their injuries and granting them a three-week medical leave, were filing a complaint against him for assault and battery.

The ring tone confirmed that the number was still active.

He found the long beeps stressful.

After a dozen rings, the Japanese greeting came, soft and reassuring: *"Kon-nichiwa."*

"Shinji Saiko?"

*"Hai . . ."*

"*Salam Aleik*, Shinji Saiko!"

Tahar's student recognized his voice, and the two men eagerly plunged into conversation, happy to hear from one another once again.

They talked for a while. They brought up shared memories and described their paths since those happy bygone days. They had both lived through a lot at their respective ends of the world. Nearly one year ago to the day, Tahar had been confined to his home with his family, respecting, like the rest of the country, a military curfew established following weeks of postrevolutionary unrest and a wave of assassinations. Shinji Saiko had been confined with his family as well, in the basement this time, respecting a radioactivity alert triggered by the tsunami that had ravaged the nuclear power plant of Fukushima, fearful of black rain falling down on them.

"Here, strong collective choices were made. Life first! The last nuclear power plant will be closed within a year."

"Here, weak collective choices were made. Death prowls every-where, among men and insects alike."

"What . . . ?"

Tahar explained the main reason for his call. He told Shinji the story of Sidi's bees, then mentioned Jannet's firm desire to go all the way to Japan.

"What a wonderful idea!" Shinji exclaimed.

"Yes, at least I think so," replied Tahar. "Shinji, would you be our guide during our trip? I'd be incapable of finding a queen bee breeder here, let alone in Japan."

"Professor, allow me to offer you my aid and my hospitality!"

# 26

"Douda, come out of your shithole."

The call wasn't clear. The voice just a nocturnal murmur, barely perceptible amid the whispering wind, howling wolves, and snoring of his pregnant wife lying next to him. But for having long awaited it, Douda heard the voice and got up. It was his friend, a brother from a different womb, as he liked to say.

He didn't believe his ears, and still he ventured out quietly, careful not to wake Hadda. As his eyes struggled to adjust to the darkness on this moonless night, he made out Toumi's shadow in front of his home. He hurried over, arms open, and the two men exchanged a long hug. Douda felt the cold of iron between their bodies and the whiskers of an abundant beard on his friend's cheeks.

"Toumi, where were you? I've been really worried!"

"I'm back. You knew, right? Tell me that you knew!"

Douda didn't know a thing. He hadn't had any news in three months and had been worried sick, but in the grip of emotion, he said, "I knew. I knew."

The two friends let go. Douda could see now and distinguish details. Toumi had changed. His barbarian beard wasn't the only new thing. His metamorphosis appeared much deeper. The many accessories complementing his black tunic attested to that: around his waist, a machete and two grenades; over his shoulder, an automatic rifle; diagonally along his torso, a large-caliber cartridge belt. Douda touched the bullets on his friend's chest.

"What happened to you, Toumi?"

"First off, don't call me Toumi anymore. Call me Abu Labba!"

"Abu what?"

"Abu Labba!"

Douda didn't understand.

"Uh, Abu meaning 'father'? Did you have a kid named Labba?"

"No, you idiot! It's my war name."

Douda could see a little farther into the deep of night and realized that his friend wasn't alone. A stone's throw behind him, between the olive trees, were a dozen bearded shadows armed with Kalashnikovs. Surprised, he took a step backward.

"Don't be afraid! I came here with my unit. That's my *katiba* there."

"War name? *Katiba*? What are you talking about, Toumi?"

"Abu Labba!" his friend growled. "The war I'm telling you about is the holy war! Have you forgotten the sermon we heard together? We're going to restore the kingdom of God to this land of unbelievers before the impending apocalypse!"

Douda was shocked. "But this isn't a land of unbelievers!"

"Yes, it is, Douda! Yes, it is! People are hypocrites. They say they belong to one religion and do the complete opposite of what it decrees. Even the Party of God makes concessions in order to rule, under the pretext of democracy. It's not radical enough. It allows communists and atheists to live. We must impose the law of God! It's time to put everyone back on the right path!"

Douda cast another glance at his friend's lethal accessories and asked him, "And you, Abu Labba, are on the right path?"

"Absolutely, Douda! I'm on the *sirat*!"

Douda looked down.

"Trust me! You'll see that I'm right soon enough. Now listen to me. How's Hadda doing? Is the pregnancy going okay?"

"Yeah."

"Here, buy her some real sea bream!" he said, slipping something into his friend's hand. Douda felt a thick wad.

"Where'd you get this?"

"God gives to those who take His path."

"So God gave you this money?"

Toumi insisted. "Take it and buy her some real sea bream and anything she wants until she delivers. Your child won't have an ill-fated life, you hear me, Douda?!"

Douda was taken aback. What fate could you promise a child brought into a world of grenades and submachine guns?

Toumi prodded his friend's chin up and placed a second wad in his hand. "Listen carefully, Douda! I'm heading to the mountains with my *katiba*. We're going to set up our camp there. Take this money and go into the village. Get some groceries for me. Buy sugar, coffee, tea, rice, pasta, potatoes, some canned food. As much as you can load onto your mule's back. Be discreet. No one can know that we're up there. We'll meet at the spring in two nights. Okay?"

Douda remained silent. Toumi shook him by the shoulders. "Okay?"

"Okay."

"Now tell me, how's Baya?"

"I don't know."

"What do you mean, you don't know?"

"She left a month ago to work in the capital."

Abu Labba's eyes gleamed in the night. "Soon the capital will fall. Soon I'll get her back."

"You guys want to bring down the capital?"

"Right into our hands, with the help of God! We're going to restore His kingdom, from the Far East to the Far West. Our brothers in Iraq and the Levant have begun the conquest. We have a caliph, Douda! Did you know that? We have a caliph, like in the golden age!"

Toumi hugged him again, then let go and retreated to rejoin his *katiba*. Their shadows were quickly swallowed up by the darkness, leaving Douda stunned, mute, frozen in place.

"In two nights, Douda. At the spring. Everything your mule can carry."

# 27

Within the week, Tahar had requested time off from the university and Jannet had freed up the pilgrimage money. She bought two tickets for Japan. The administrative formalities, which they had stumbled on for every previous trip, were less complicated than they feared. In fact, the Japanese government didn't demand an entry visa for citizens from their country. You simply crossed the border with a valid passport.

"That doesn't surprise me," commented Tahar. "Who from here would go so far away?"

"Us!" Jannet answered with delight.

A few days later, they were aboard a long-haul aircraft heading to Tokyo.

They held hands for the whole trip. They had traveled separately before. Now, they were taking the plane together for the first time.

One layover and twenty hours later, they arrived in the Japanese capital. They had slept for much of the flight and woke when the plane was beginning its descent. They admired the sprawling archipelago from the window. The landscape was like nothing they'd seen. Hundreds of islands scattered across the ocean, with verdant flora and countless volcanoes and hills. As the plane descended lower, they made out rice fields gleaming in the setting sun, and farther away, cities stretching between mountains and ocean.

The bright Haneda airport was so efficiently organized that it only took them fifteen minutes to go through border control. Once the formalities were complete, they found their luggage had already been sent to a conveyer belt.

"Unbelievable!"

"What?"

"The twenty minutes between an international flight landing and us leaving the airport," he replied, pushing a luggage cart.

In the arrivals hall, a man in casual attire was waiting for them with a sign written in Arabic: Tahar and Jannet.

"Is that Shinji?" whispered Jannet.

"Yes, it is," answered Tahar.

"I thought he'd be younger than you," she whispered.

"He's almost ten years older! Back then, I was younger than most of my students."

With a broad smile, Shinji advanced to meet them, and the two men warmly shook hands. Shinji spoke in slightly rusty Arabic.

"Professor Tahar! What a joy to see you again."

"After all these years. And without hara-kiri," joked Tahar. "Allow me to introduce the instigator of our trip, my wife, Jannet."

"Jannet! I'm so honored," said Shinji, bowing repeatedly.

"The honor is all mine!"

"My wife is waiting impatiently for you. Follow me. My car is parked on the basement level."

Jannet complimented their host during the drive.

"Mr. Saiko, your Arabic merits admiration."

"Well, that's because I had a good professor! A good professor!" he repeated as if to double-check his words.

"You were a brilliant student. The only punctual one," recalled Tahar.

"I've been studying a lot since your call," he laughed, before continuing, "Professor, one day you asked me what Japan was like. You're going to see for yourself."

Looking out the window, Tahar was already immersed in the lights of Tokyo. Shinji made sure to drive slowly, giving him time to observe the landscape. The city streamed by before his awestruck gaze. It wasn't as cluttered as he had imagined but actually gave the feeling of space thanks to its wide roads. The buildings varied in height and the neighborhoods in density. Impressive skyscrapers on the outskirts of the city gave way to low buildings adorned with giant screens and signs, hosting boutiques, bars, and restaurants in which the nightlife was just awakening.

"Tokyo endured terrible bombings during World War II. Nearly the entire city was rebuilt."

The residential neighborhoods far from the center were markedly calmer, like Itabashi, where Shinji and his wife, Inoue, lived alone. Grandparents for a few years now, they too were questioning the future of their grandchildren and the world they would leave them.

Opening the door, Inoue bowed to them and they followed suit. She repeated several warm phrases in her language.

Shinji served as interpreter. "She welcomes you to our home!"

"It's a pleasure to meet you, and thank you for welcoming us," they answered.

In keeping with Japanese tradition, they removed their shoes at the entryway and put on slippers. Although small, the Saikos' house was comfortable: the space was mastered and optimized as best it could be. Everything was tighter than the standard to which Tahar and Jannet were accustomed. Even the indoor plants had been adjusted to minimalist dimensions.

"Those are bonsai plants, miniature trees. They require care and particular attention," explained Shinji.

Before leaving them to rest in the guest room, Shinji took Tahar aside and warned him, in all seriousness: "Professor, you will notice that there are several buttons in the bathroom that generate multiple sprays of water. Do not panic. Trust your instinct."

# 28

"A delicious mix of modernity and tradition. How very true . . . ," repeated Tahar as he was exposed to Japanese culture.

And exposed he was, during the small discovery tour Shinji, hoping to enrich his guests' short visit, had designed for them.

Early in the morning, he brought them to Tokyo's famous tuna auction. At the insistence of Shinji and the fish seller, Tahar and Jannet reluctantly swallowed pieces of raw fish before joyfully taking seconds.

At the ancestral temple of Asakusa, the Sensō-ji, they were lucky enough to observe a prayer recited by Buddhist monks, whose chanting was echoed by devoted followers. They wandered through the temple's Zen gardens, whose ponds boasted carp serenely floating near the water's surface.

One evening, near the Sumida River, they dined in a *ryōtei*, a traditional restaurant, where they watched a show of songs and fan dances performed by apprentice geisha. "You're not in your glass house anymore!" And Tahar no longer knew, as he finished his sentence, whether he was talking about the geisha or himself.

They visited the electric neighborhood of Akihabara by night, observing the light-drenched buildings, amped-up gamers, and stream of oddly dressed figures walking by.

"They're disguised as manga characters. They identify with them. It's a massive phenomenon in Japan," noted Shinji about these fantastical looks.

At Ueno Park, after coming across a few sumo wrestlers, their staggering corpulence contained by immaculate kimonos, triggering hysteria and veneration in their wake, they stumbled upon a troop of fake Elvises, who were improvising rock 'n' roll dances around vintage speakers.

All these men and women looked different, and yet their expressions were very familiar. Courteous and united by respect for the rules of the community.

Tahar noted his astonishment in his journal.

> *Over the past two days I've seen large men line up behind small men to enter the metro and trains that are always on time. I've seen pedestrians stopping at red lights even at midnight when there's not a single car around. I've seen streets and parks so clean they sparkle. Not a piece of paper or cigarette butt on the ground. In the temples and Zen gardens, they take care of everything down to the fallen petals, which are gathered in small piles beneath the flowers.*

His palate acclimated, Tahar enthusiastically dug into his nightly ramen.

"How did you reach this degree of civility, Mrs. Saiko?"

She responded slowly, giving her husband time to translate: "Like our bees that have to coexist with the giant hornets, we are a people who must coexist with the flaws in the earth—earthquakes, tsunamis, volcanic eruptions—and with war, the flaw of human nature. We know that our archipelago is fragile, that our existence is fragile, and that the survivors must always rebuild. We are a people well versed in catastrophes,

Professor. The 'other' is none other than ourselves, a survivor and a partner.

"However," she continued, "you shouldn't idealize Japanese society either. It's secretive and hides many peculiarities that are difficult for foreigners to grasp."

Jannet didn't dare tell them about her mishap that day. As they were strolling through Shibuya, she'd seen a window displaying schoolgirl uniforms. She naively entered the store, to her immediate regret. There were definitely schoolgirl uniforms, but also nurse uniforms, stewardess uniforms . . . Blow-up dolls and sex toys, from the highly suggestive to the crudest, filled the aisles of this multistory boutique. She ran out, reciting a few prayers, wondering how such seemingly timid people could frequent such places.

# 29

High up in the Tokyo Skytree, Tahar was dumbstruck. Walled in entirely by glass, this floor offered a grandiose panorama of the entire Japanese capital.

Standing at the base of the tallest freestanding tower in the world, Jannet had already felt dizzy. When she tried to make out the very top, she almost fell backward. The LEDs grafted to the neofuturistic structure emitted an elegant blue glow that enhanced its slender metallic skeleton.

The elevators that went up to the Tembo Deck, a 360-degree observation platform, took less than one minute to transport visitors, and Tahar had to be especially persuasive to convince his wife to go up with him.

"Can you imagine if the elevator falls and I die alone?"

But the elevator was a cocoon, and despite the lightning ascent, they didn't feel a single jolt. Vertigo gave way to amazement.

They found themselves on the 350th floor, over one thousand feet above the ground. It was after ten p.m., and as they watched, Tokyo unveiled its architectural prowess and imperial ways. Multicolored nocturnal lights created a halo over the metropolis that stretched beyond the horizon. Skyscrapers punctuated the landscape like columns of light. The colossal city structure extended as far as the eye could see, straddling the inlets of Tokyo Bay and shooting out in every direction its precise and spacious tentacles—roads, railway tracks, and bridges on which trains and cars were weaving like toys decorated with tinsel. As they admired the view, they listened to Shinji's voice untangling the urban expanse for them.

"In front, that's Yokohama City. Farther off, that's Odaiba Island. Mount Fuji is to the west. It's not visible at night. Nikkō is two hours away in that direction."

"That's where the queen breeder is?"

"That's right," said Shinji, nodding. "That's where we're going tomorrow."

"*Inshallah,*" added Jannet to herself.


The village of Nikkō hadn't been abandoned, like Nawa and the other villages back home. On the contrary, it was a crown jewel proud of its temples, which included Tōshō-gū, home to the three "hear no evil, see no evil, speak no evil" monkeys of wisdom and the sleeping cat, symbol of kindness toward the weak, as well as Rinnō-ji and its famous golden Buddhas who incarnate the sacred mountains of Nikkō.

Shinji parked the car near the train station, and the group continued on foot through small, peaceful streets studded by small houses with manicured lawns. They took a path that led to the bee farm.

Shinji walked in front, and his two guests followed hand in hand. They hadn't been hiking in years. But behind Shinji, mesmerized by the dazzling landscape, Jannet had forgotten all about her arthritis and Tahar his back pain. It was the height of spring and everywhere cherry trees were blossoming, shining with green and ruby. After passing beneath the torii, the gates separating the sacred from the worldly, they walked beside a crystalline river that originated in the high, mountainous peaks. Reinvigorated by the snow thaw, it was guarded by meditating stone Buddhas all along its course. Tahar, who'd been robbed on three occasions, noticed the small piles of money placed by supplicants below the statues, which waited, without fear, to be collected by the monks.

Nature was playing them a harmonious score of falling water, birdsong, and crackling branches, and as they went deeper, they heard bees buzzing, joining the soothing concert. Soon, they saw them at work, skipping from flower to flower. The closer they got, the more bees abounded. Small golden orbs beating their wings and gleaming beneath the sun. The trio had reached their destination. Buildings emerged from the valleys in front of them; the bee farm looked like a temple.

"There it is," shouted Shinji, pointing.

"We're here!" cheered Jannet.

A few more steps and they found themselves at the entrance to the farmstead, welcomed by its owner, Kisuke Ukitake, in a white kimono and wooden sandals. His face was a study in kindness and restraint but it also revealed his emotion at seeing suitors for his girls come from so far. Hands joined beneath his chin, this man of indeterminable age made a long bow. They returned the greeting.

"Welcome to my humble farm."

"It's a joy and an honor for us."

"If you'll follow me, please."

Kisuke Ukitake took them on a tour of the apicultural domain, telling them its history as they walked. Though sprawling, with thousands of colonies, the property, established by his ancestors in the seventeenth century, remained a family business. Today, he was the director and guardian of tradition. He would transmit his knowledge to his grandchildren and teach them, before he died, the art of maintaining life.

The trees were dotted with hives, and the bees, God's beauties, were working at great haste on this spring day. Observing the beekeeper walk, talk in a melodious voice, and caress his girls, Jannet couldn't help but think of Sidi. The resemblance was striking. They had the same silhouette, the same gestures, and the same love in their voices.

Like brothers from a single, unique mother, she mused—Mother Nature.

At the end of the tour, Kisuke Ukitake brought them inside and served them matcha. The queens were ready, placed individually in aerated Plexiglas cages the size of pocket dictionaries, accompanied by their bodyguards, who would feed them with the honey stored in their bellies. Tahar and Jannet stared in fascination at the *Apis japonica*, black as coal, pacing in their boxes, driven by their desire to join a hive. Soon they would cross oceans to bring the knowledge coded in their genes.

Shinji spoke first. "When I explained the reasons for your journey to Ukitake-sama, he refused payment."

"I can't accept money," said the beekeeper. "This is a gift. Offer these queens to the man who seeks them. In his eyes, they have no price. These are good empresses. Don't wait long before putting them to work."


That night, as he was packing, Tahar was only able to squeeze in nineteen of the twenty boxes. One queen wouldn't fit in his luggage.

"Give her to me," suggested Jannet. "Hello, my dear," she said. "You and I are going to be traveling together!"

And she carefully placed the queen in her bag.

# 30

"So, Professor, what do you think of Japan?"

"I learned more about myself here than I did about Japan," answered Tahar.

In the plane, he squeezed Jannet's hand. "Thank you for this wonderful trip."

"You see . . . you were right to come."

After twenty hours in the air and one layover, they landed beneath a familiar blue sky. The plane hadn't reached its berth yet but the passengers were already standing up with their luggage, elbowing their way through the narrow aisles to exit the aircraft first.

"We're definitely home," laughed Tahar.

At border control, there weren't enough agents to handle the multiheaded queues, and a few altercations broke out sporadically between shameless line cutters and those they offended. Finally, it was Tahar and Jannet's turn. The agent examined their passports, gave them a hard look, then consulted a list. He addressed Tahar: "Are you the Tahar M. that's the dean of the College of Arts and Sciences?"

"Yes."

"You're his wife?"

"Yes."

He stamped Jannet's passport and returned it to her, then grabbed his telephone handset and made a short call. Once two men had joined him at his station, he stated: "Ma'am, move forward, please. Sir, the public prosecutor has issued a warrant for you. You're under arrest."

The couple exchanged an incredulous look.

"What's going on? What am I being accused of?" asked Tahar, in shock.

"Calm down!" ordered an agent.

"Follow us. We'll explain," said the other.

"I'm not leaving without my husband!" protested Jannet.

Tahar knew that the police still had a quick hand. The revolution hadn't revolutionized backward mentalities. He tried to reassure his wife, whispering in her ear, "Don't worry. Go home and call a lawyer!"

Then he turned back to the wolves. "Let's go, gentlemen."

He disappeared into the airport's labyrinth escorted by men in uniform.

Tahar left the airport like a repeat offender: passport, cell phone, and suitcase confiscated. He was immediately placed in a small van with a siren and brought before the public prosecutor.

The man across from him was in his thirties, sporting a trimmed beard and a black suit and tie. He was holding the dean's passport and looked very serious. Tahar noted that there were no windows in the office and that his luggage was set on a table, surrounded by three officers.

"Do you know why you're here?"

"I don't."

"Really? That's what you're claiming? Well, then allow me to refresh your memory."

Fists glued to the table, the public prosecutor was tapping his index fingers frenetically, like a hornet clicking his jaws.

"Two weeks ago, you assaulted two of your female students and pushed them down the stairs at the university. Two students who came to you to voice a collective desire regarding how the institution functions."

Tahar's eyes opened wide. "That's an untruthful claim. I never did what you're accusing me of!"

The police officers standing around his things glared at him.

"Well, let's see!" continued the inquisitor. "I have right here a medical certificate that attests to their injuries and grants them a twenty-day leave from classes due to their total incapacity to work. Do you think they got those bruises and fractures all by themselves in their sleep?"

"Of course not. They were perfectly conscious when they threw themselves down the stairs as they left my office. They didn't need to be pushed!"

"So you admit you received them in your office!"

"I'm not denying that!"

"And you don't deny that you refused to grant their requests?" the prosecutor continued.

"And how was I supposed to grant their requests? We can't separate genders and stop classes during prayer time! It's impossible!"

"Why is that, Professor? Why exactly is it impossible? Are such demands really so unfounded? Mightn't you be an *ilmani*?"

Everyone looked at Tahar. What the prosecutor said was true. If he was a man of science, was he not then hostile to religion?

"That's not the reason for my arrest. I'm not here to discuss the university charter with you. And your accusations are grotesque!"

"You underestimate our case, Professor. I have here damning eyewitness accounts against you."

"Eyewitnesses? The only witness at the scene was my vice-dean."

"Your vice-dean is also under arrest for assault and battery. He's been in temporary custody for three days. And there were in fact other

witnesses at the scene. Students, who saw everything! All their state-
ments are included in the case file," he said, waving a folder in the air.

"What? Three days? Other witnesses? Have you lost your mind?"

"Careful what you say, Professor. The charges leveled against you are
serious," warned the prosecutor firmly. "What were you doing in Japan?
Perhaps you were trying to forget what happened?"

"Forget? After one week? Really? You can't be serious!"

"Spare me your commentaries and answer! What were you doing
in Japan?"

"It's a private matter."

"You no longer have any privacy. Unpack his things," he ordered.

The three police officers, immobile until then, opened the suitcase. They removed clothes, books, and, one by one, the nineteen royal
vessels.

"What are those?" said the prosecutor in shock when he saw the
insects in their mini cages.

"Those are bees," answered Tahar.

"So you are unaware, Professor, that the introduction of undeclared
living species is strictly forbidden and subject to punishment?"

"With the exception of bees, leeches, and silkworms," corrected
Tahar. "And these insects are bees."

"Bees, you say? Hmm, I see flies. Officers, what do you see?"

"Flies!"

"They're bees! I have the documents to prove it." Tahar hurriedly
reached into his jacket and removed papers stamped by Kisuke, written
in Japanese and English, and unfolded them before his accuser.

The prosecutor grabbed one, skimmed it, then immediately passed
it back.

"The thing is, we don't have any translators, so your papers are of no
use at all. And we can't take the risk of allowing you to liberate these flies
into nature. Only God knows what kind of plague they could spread. Is

that it? Your plan for the country, *ilmani*? Unleash the plague? Officers, destroy these flies!"

Tahar tried to block them with his body but he was immediately, and professionally, pummeled with batons. While two of the officers restrained him by the shoulders, the third lined up the nineteen carriers on the floor. Then he raised his foot nineteen times and crushed them one by one with a grime-covered boot. The delicate bodies yielded under the large sole.

"Stop! Stop! Those bees are our future!"

After the nineteenth slaughter, his jailers released his shoulders and he fell to his knees in front of the tiny cages and the flattened corpses of the dead queens.

"Bastards! You bastards!" cried Tahar in tears, aching in both body and soul.

"Insult to acting officers of the law. We'll add that to the list of your offenses," gloated the prosecutor. Then he leaned over Tahar, and scratched his beard with a learned air: "*Ilmani*, you truly are a man without faith. Our future isn't in your luggage. Our future is in the hands of God!"


In front of the Ministry of the Interior, Jannet and her children were losing patience. Tahar had been held there since the night before, and they'd had no news. They didn't even know what he was being accused of, and only his lawyer, a friend of the family, had obtained the right to visit him.

"How is he?"

Having been lectured by Tahar, Mr. Ferjeni was careful not to mention his bruises to Jannet.

"He's fine, don't worry. We'll get him out of here by tomorrow."

"But what are they accusing him of?"

"Assaulting students."

"Assaulting students? That's ridiculous!"

"Of course it's ridiculous! Everyone knows that. I can promise you that he'll be free tomorrow morning, after the detention period is up. But Jannet, one more thing."

"Yes?"

The lawyer seemed nonplussed. He was afraid that his friend was a bit unhinged after his beating and had given him an incoherent message to deliver. He continued, "Tahar wants you to know that they murdered the queens and that you have to deliver the last hope to Nawa. Umm . . . what does that mean?"

# THE AFTERMATH

## Sidi's Song

*Here below, I continue to walk and to read*
*In the ruins I search where your footprints lead*
*So clear and distinct once the chaos recedes*
*I wield the darkness, and you the light*
*You are my haven as I continue this fight*

# 31

Sidi stood still before the mountain.

Decades earlier, it had been a nature reserve, its flora and fauna cataloged and protected, its hiking trails marked and maintained. Today, the mountain was abandoned, and only an expert or fugitive would dare venture within.

The giant hornets were there, lying in wait in the brush, and he had no choice but to find their nests and neutralize them before a new attack came.

He knew his preventive strategy was far from a permanent solution.

"God only knows how many nests there are. It'd be presumptuous to say we'd gotten all of them. But that's no reason to sit on our hands."

He took a deep breath and pulled on his mule's bridle. "Come on, Staka, we've got work to do."

The week had gone by without incident.

Sidi's Nawi backup showed up every morning and kept watch while he scoured the neighboring fields and scrubland without finding any trace of the beasts. When he had announced to the villagers his intention to explore the mountain, Douda took him aside.

"Don't go!" he implored.

"But I have to."

"It's dangerous," Douda choked out, weighed down by his secret.

Sidi remembered his confrontation with the hornets and the aggressiveness they had displayed in battle, but that didn't dissuade him. He folded his double ladder and loaded it in his cart next to his tools and his white beekeeper suit.

"Don't worry."

He was ready.

Flushing out a nest of hornets in the mountains might have been an uncertain undertaking, but only if one didn't take into account the plan he had devised to improve his chances. A simple plan he hoped would be effective. He was well aware that hornets can pick up the smell of honey from miles in all directions. He had what he needed to lure them.

As he left the steppe, he heard, as he had during his last expedition, the sounds of engines and tires coming up the road. The convoy of border guards finally came into view, and once again it matched its speed to his donkey's. He still felt like he was seeing children in shrouds.

He recognized the young soldiers, and the same one addressed him. This time, he said, "Morning, sir!"

Now that's much better, thought Sidi.

"Morning," he responded.

"You going hunting?" asked the captain.

"I'm not going poaching, if that's what you mean."

"Be careful out there!"

"You too."

The cars raced off.

The heat was scorching on this April day, flooding the air with the smell of pine and brush and panicking the insects whizzing by.

Staka was pulling the small cart behind his master. Sidi was leading the way, paying attention to the smallest detail, drawing on each of his senses, ears perked, scanning his surroundings. He entered the heart of the mountain and began to ascend. As they advanced, he spotted footprints on recently treaded paths. A few cigarette butts crushed in food cans.

"Bipeds," he muttered, bowing to the evidence.

He had a bad feeling and soon changed direction.

"Let's head right, Staka."

The donkey followed without protest, Sidi still leading the way, taking side paths. When he judged they were at the right height, he looked for a spot to set up his trap and chose a small shaded plateau.

"Stop, little Staka!"

The donkey stopped, flicking its ears. Sidi unloaded his tools and changed his clothes. He took his red *kabbus* off his head and removed his blue polyester jacket, slipped on his white beekeeper suit, and displayed his bait: a small wooden crate in which he had placed an entire honeycomb frame, taken from one of his hives. He set it down, wide open.

"Come on out. I'm waiting . . ."

But very quickly other insects picked up the smell of honey. He immediately chased them away. "Shoo! This isn't for you."

The wait was trying. Minutes turned into hours during which he battled every insect around except the ones he had come to track. His reason and intuition finally persuaded him that he was on the wrong side of the mountain, so he put away the honeycomb, loaded the cart, and summoned his partner.

"Come on, Staka, let's go."

The small cortege moved on.


By dusk, Sidi was on the right side of the mountain, facing the border and the western wind. After a day beneath the cloak of the hot sun, the forest was groggy and sweating. Both he and the donkey were exhausted. In order to make it here, they'd had to abandon the cart and climb up the mountain slope like a pair of bucks.

He set up camp, gave Staka some water, and made a bed for himself. He took off his shoes and knelt before the fire. Suffering from a headache and a few knots in his back, he massaged his head, pressing on his temples, and stretched his muscles and old bones. It had been a wearing week, but this wasn't the moment to succumb to the consequences.

Before falling asleep under the stars, he ate his fill and drank until he was quenched, did his ablutions, and prayed to God, the God of bees, the God of books, to guide him, to grant him luck, and to place His strength and His wisdom in his hands.

The next morning, he woke before sunrise and warmed up his limbs.

From his new position on the border side, Sidi took out his bait and began the same wait as the day before.

This time, it wasn't tiresome but brief and fruitful. Midmorning, he heard a distinctive, bloodcurdling sound. A heavy buzzing that filled the air and drowned out everything else.

"They're here!"

Two giant hornets emerged from the brush flying in formation. They confidently moved into the open, sure of their supremacy, cleaving the air with their enormous wings like two bomber planes. Once level with the crate, they carried out a stationary observation flight before beginning landing maneuvers. They settled on the edge of the box.

"Yes, good, now mark it," said Sidi, observing them attentively.

The two hornets strutted along the walls of the lure, shaking their bodies, spreading their scent. Once their dance was complete, as they were preparing to take off, Sidi caught the larger one by its wings while its partner resumed flight.

"Freeze!"

Like the last time, the captive hornet displayed tremendous aggressiveness. Trapped between Sidi's fingers, it nervously twitched its hairy feet, clicked its jaws over and over, and frenetically extended and retracted its stinger.

"Calm down. I'll let you go in a second."

He took a thin red ribbon from his pocket, which he carefully tied around the creature's giant abdomen.

"Here. Now I can track you."

Before releasing his captive, Sidi cleaned the crate and closed it, then addressed his donkey: "Don't move, I'll be back."

He opened his fingers and the hornet immediately flew away, trailing the little ribbon in the sky. Sidi ran after, not letting it out of his sight, marking the trees with a piece of chalk along the way.

"Lead me, but not too quick! I don't have the legs of a twenty-year-old anymore."

Handicapped by the marker encumbering its wings, the insect lost speed and stopped several times on the way to its nest. Yet Sidi, hustling behind, still had trouble keeping up.

A breathless half hour of scrambling over hedges and vines later, the hunt ended at the foot of a dizzying pine tree some fifty feet high. The insect labored to reach the top, where a nest was suspended like a giant chandelier. Sidi watched the creature ascend and let out a long whistle. "Well, well. There must be thousands of hornets in that thing! And this double ladder isn't going to do much to help me get to them."

He judged the nest's diameter to be around three feet and guessed at its weight. Dislodging the hornets' home and bringing it down would be a perilous undertaking. Aware that he was at the limit of what a man even in his prime could accomplish, Sidi, bold, didn't waver.

"It's still within your reach, old man."

And if failure proved to be fatal, then His will be done. Sidi believed that every man had his hour, and he wasn't going to wait for his beneath the shade of an olive tree. He was acting for the sake of his girls, whatever the cost. He returned to his camp and came back with his tools and Staka as backup.

He spent the rest of the day observing his adversaries, analyzing their behavior, and studying how their fortress was situated. It was perfectly sealed, with a single hatch on the lower half allowing access.

He circled the pine tree several times like a mountaineer nervous about an ascent. He carefully studied its winding trunk, dense and solid foliage, and large crown hanging like a parasol.

"You see, Staka, I'm going to do something that you've never seen me do because in all my life, I've never done it. I'm going to climb this tree to that massive nest. I'm going to dislodge it and bring it back down. If I fall and break my neck, I'm counting on you to carry my body back to the house and organize a lovely funeral."

Staka flicked his ears and gazed at his master cheerfully, as if saying, "Don't worry about that and get climbing already!"

"Going after the nest by day would be suicide, but so would climbing this tree at night," he admitted.

"What are you planning to do?"

"Two birds, one stone," responded Sidi. "At dawn, I'll have some visibility and they'll still be asleep. That's when we'll surprise them."

He camped out a few feet away, biding his time, finishing his preparations. He diluted clay powder in water and worked the mixture until he had a soft dough.

Clay from clay, he thought. Knead, knead. Knead what you were and what you will be. Knead, knead, while you're still alive!

Under a star-studded dome, as the crescent moon got lost behind a few clouds, Sidi too felt lost, asking himself the ultimate question, for which he found no answer.

Was he a just man?

He eventually fell asleep, and his sleep was soothed by a lovely dream in which his girls were happy, dancing in hives transformed into celebrating villages. Not even the appearance of a hornet scout with a hideous beard could ruin the fun. No panic! Maestro, more music, please! The bees, joyful as ever, jumped on the intruder, formed a ball, and merged their bodies to form a blazing red ruby of unrivaled brightness, so hot it reduced the unwanted guest to ashes.

But though this dream remained lodged in his unconscious, he gained no lessons from it. He gained nothing but a restful sleep, necessary for his plans for the following day.

# 32

Dawn was making its entrance in the sky and between the mosque minarets, illuminating beautiful Venus and prompting the muezzins to call out, when Sidi began to pray in his fashion. He slipped on his white suit and beekeeper helmet, wrapped a sheet and a rope around one shoulder, and hung the heavy bag of clay dough around his neck. He wedged his donkey against the tree and hoisted himself onto his back to climb the first branches. He nearly tumbled down a few times, unstable on the wet bark. Below his feet, Staka was watching as if to encourage him to continue the ascent.

Everything was silent. There was just his internal voice urging him to give it his all. He had no idea that lower down the mountain, a commander was urging Toumi and the members of his *katiba* to destroy the patrol of border guards.

"My brothers! Today is a blessed day. Today we declare war on this state that refuses the law of God and observes its colonial borders. This morning, we will put our training and our plan into action. We will attack this patrol of apostates! We will exterminate every last one of them! God is great!"

"God is great!"

"God is great!"

Inside his protective armor, Sidi advanced slowly and reached the top of the tree without waking the monsters. Face-to-face with their nest, he was even more impressed by its size and outer bark: a true fortress for a huge colony.

"Nice work. But this masterpiece must have a flaw."

He examined the surface and found the breach.

Holding his breath, he grabbed a handful of clay from his bag and took a step, but almost fell.

"Careful! You're almost there."

He tried again, and this time he was able to coordinate his movements and plug the hatch. He took a breath. Then he added another layer of clay.

"This'll stop you coming out . . ."


The next stage was more delicate.

Perched on his high branch, Sidi placed his hands on the hornet fortress. Its walls were sturdy, which reassured him. He grabbed the nest and, in one motion, detached it. It was heavy, much heavier than expected. He nearly dropped it and for a second imagined the nest tumbling to the ground, breaking, and being his ruin. But he resisted. He resisted the weight of his years and the weight of the hornets and managed to stay upright, leaning against the trunk, as he wedged his troubling prize in front of him, in the thick foliage. Despite his precarious balance, he immediately began coating the entire nest with the clay mixture to better contain the calamity it held.

When he was done, he wrapped the nest in the sheet, then wound the rope around it like a net, which he lowered very, very gently.

His back and arms were rudely tested, but his will and steady hands didn't weaken.

Once the nest was on the ground, a breathless Sidi released the rope.

"Now it's my turn to return to dry land," he panted.


Coming down from such a tree was as dangerous as climbing it, and he was starting this final stage with only the meager energy he had remaining. He gauged the void beneath his unsteady feet and after taking a large breath, he began.

"Come what may!"

Alternating between a kind of rappel and crisscrossing side steps, he finally set his feet on the hard soil, where he collapsed. Staka came over and sniffed him.

"Bravo, old friend! You see, I didn't have to organize your funeral after all."

His master remained motionless for a second, recovering from his efforts.

But Sidi was unable to savor his victory.

Sitting across from the clay-engulfed nest, which looked more like a tomb, he wondered what he would do with it now that he'd doomed its inhabitants.

Would he let his enemies suffocate to death?

Though basic logic was telling him to do just that, the idea struck him as indefensible. Who did he take himself for, thinking he could eradicate them just like that?

What was his true role in this story? Beekeeper or God?

His whole life, he had restricted himself to the former, a role in which he found fulfillment. He had raised his girls, breeding into them the behaviors necessary for their survival and defense. If only he could teach them the ardent swarm. If only he was a queen capable of imparting that precious secret.

But only a queen had that gift. He was merely a man, and his duty was to destroy. A nest of hornets, but living hornets. Was duty the only solution?

The question was sparking a crisis of conscience.

"Oh God, help me be good!"

He removed his helmet and attached it to his belt. He placed the nest on Staka's back, stabilizing it with ropes, then pulled on the bridle. He had the whole way back to debate with his inner voices and resolve his moral dilemma.

"Come on, Staka. We're going home. I don't have the strength to get the cart. We'll come back tomorrow."

They descended the side of the mountain so they could reach the road and return to Nawa.

They were only a few feet above the path that ran along the border when Sidi noticed the three patrol jeeps below him. They were conducting their morning round in single file, and as he watched, they leaned into a narrow turn. He continued to descend the slope, deep in thought, when an extraordinary noise interrupted his rumination, causing Staka to rear back far enough to knock Sidi to the ground. He stood up, a little dazed, and witnessed the scene.

The border guards had just entered an ambush.

A powerful homemade bomb exploded under the last jeep in the convoy. Catapulted into the air, gas tank ablaze, the vehicle landed roof down and transformed into a ball of fire.

Taken by surprise, the two jeeps in the lead braked abruptly. That's when the *katiba* lying in wait burst out, in front and from the sides, screaming that God is great. Fifteen men began emptying their

Kalashnikovs and tossing grenades into the first two jeeps blocked by the third one in flames.

The narrowness of the bend rendered all maneuvers to escape or reverse hopeless, and the vehicles collided.

The attackers continued to close their trap. They slowly advanced on the patrol, firing steadily. Automatic weapons spit out death at high speed. Bullets riddled windows and sheet metal and ripped apart flesh and bones. The ground was drenched in crimson.

After several minutes, the shooting stopped and the monsters' voices thundered out.

"Victory! Victory!"

"God is great!"

"God is great!"

Sidi could hear them from where he was standing. But what God were they worshipping?

Toumi and his comrades opened the battered car doors. Inside, a blood-bath of mutilated bodies. All the patrol guards had been hit by several large-caliber shots, and a few had been dismembered. Some had taken a bullet in the head and died instantly. Others were taking their final breaths on the jeep seats.

The commander took out a camera and turned it on.

"Slit every one of their throats!" he ordered.

Inside the frame, Toumi and the others laid the bodies stomach down, stood behind them, holding their victims by the scalp, and took out long knives.

Toumi had ended up with a dying guard. When he took him by the hair, he glimpsed a bloodied face and eyes flirting with death. He was like Toumi, in the spring of life, barely a reed, soon to be cut. Toumi shut his eyes. He didn't want to look at his victim. He pressed the knife against his throat.

"Abu Bouk, now you're going to unfurl the black flag behind them. Wait for me to give the order. I don't have you all in the frame," said the commander, walking back a few steps. He was focused on his screen, and once he was satisfied with the shot, he began to record. "Today, on this day of glory, thanks to God, we . . ."

But he was interrupted by a figure that appeared in the background. He looked up and saw an old man dressed in white coming toward them, carrying a large jar made of clay.

"Where'd he come from?" he said before shouting, "Who are you?"

Startled by this improbable presence, everyone froze. Sidi stopped between the jeep in flames and the other vehicles, now metal sieves, amid pools of flesh and blood, here where men were about to slit the throats of other men.

In his hands, animals driven by instinct, and across from him, humans driven by free will. Among these creatures mired in clay, who were the true monsters?

He felt devastated . . .


He recognized Toumi, who was skirting his gaze, despite his neolithic beard and blood-splattered face. He was holding a dying soldier by the scalp. Sidi recognized him too. It was the guard who had spoken to him during his patrols. He wouldn't be able to do so ever again. He would no longer address him as either *haj* or sir. Soon he would die, like his comrades, killed before their time, young lives sacrificed on the altar of the absurd.

His disgusted voice brought an end to the echoes of "God is great" still reverberating across the mountain.

"Was it God that asked you to do this, Toumi?" roared Sidi.

Toumi looked down, and the commander shouted at him, "You know this old fool?"

"Yes. I know him . . . Commander, he's just a poor villager. Let him go," he said weakly.

The commander pointed his weapon at Sidi.

"You hear that, old man? Hurry up and get out of here! We're waging holy war. War in the name of God!"

"God doesn't defeat the just, so war it is!"

With one assured motion, he smashed the nest on the ground and it split in two. Within seconds, thousands of hysterical giant hornets were everywhere. In search of vengeance since dawn, they had been waiting to be liberated to go on the attack.

Sidi undid his beekeeper helmet from his belt and protected himself from what came next.


Without warning, the giant hornets began to chase the men. In the blink of an eye, each found himself in the center of a cloud of beasts turned mad, enduring the lightning bolts of their fury. Electrified, the hornets charged en masse, covering hands and faces, latching onto tufts of beards and hair, diving into the folds of *qamis* and turbans, relentlessly stinging. The men found that the weapons they had thought so powerful were of no help to them. Run as fast as they could? Where could they go before they tripped, rolled to the ground, and succumbed to the attacks of thousands of unrivaled hunters?

In no time at all, the cries of triumph turned into cries of fear and horror, and the vanquishers were vanquished. The *katiba* was wiped out, all its members vanished in the brush, drowned in the cloud of its punishment.

Sidi brushed a few hornets off his helmet visor. He had seen enough.

He went back for Staka and took the road to the village, damning in his heart the commander, his *katiba*, and all the murderers and war-mongers prostituting God to their ends. A God that could still console him for the cruelty of man through the gentleness of his bees.

# 33

Sitting in his garden, Sidi was watching Farah run between the hives, which swarmed with new generations of bees, amused by their festive dance. She was three now. She couldn't speak very well yet, but her eyes were the most expressive in the world. She came to visit him often. When she laughed, it was difficult not to succumb to this call of joy and laugh over the elementary beauty of life along with her.

As Kisuke Ukitake promised, the surviving queen had proven to be hardworking and charismatic. He had named her Aya—"miracle" in Arabic, "wild beauty" in Japanese. When Jannet placed her in Sidi's hands, in her tiny crate, he had been so happy that his eyes shone beneath a limpid veil. "Ah, my beautiful Aya . . . Welcome to your new home!"

Using gentle movements and his apicultural expertise, he had introduced her into a hive, where she was accepted. She soon produced several generations of forager bees and new promising queens.

But had she transmitted her knowledge? Would his bees be able to defend themselves from the monsters? He didn't know.

Since their last face-off, he had captured a few hornets prowling around his colonies. But they hadn't returned in number.

Nor had he gone hunting for their nests again. He had accepted that they were there, hidden, threatening. All he hoped was that his girls would be ready the day they reemerged from the forest.

# ABOUT THE AUTHOR

*Photo © Delphine Manai*

Yamen Manai was born in 1980 in Tunis and currently lives in Paris. Both a writer and an engineer, Manai explores the intersections of past and present, and tradition and technology, in his prose. In *The Ardent Swarm* (originally published as *L'Amas ardent*), his first book to be translated into English, he celebrates Tunisia's rich oral culture, a tradition abounding in wry, often fatalistic humor. He has published three novels with the Tunisia-based Éditions Elyzad a deliberate choice to ensure that his books are accessible to Tunisian readers: *La marche de l'incertitude* (2010), awarded Tunisia's prestigious Prix Comar d'Or; *La sérénade d'Ibrahim Santos* (2011); and *L'Amas ardent* (2017), which earned both the Prix Comar d'Or and the Prix des Cinq Continents, a literary prize recognizing exceptional Francophone literature.

# ABOUT THE TRANSLATOR

*Photo © Pascal Michel*

Lara Vergnaud is a literary translator from the French. Her translations include Ahmed Bouanani's *The Hospital* (New Directions, 2018) and Zahia Rahmani's *France, Story of a Childhood* (Yale University Press, 2016), as well as works by Mohamed Leftah, Joy Sorman, and Scholastique Mukasonga, among others. Lara is the recipient of two PEN/Heim Translation Grants and a French Voices Grand Prize and has been nominated for the National Translation Award.